CW01091336

ANOTHER ANGEL

Amanda Richardson

MINERVA PRESS
LONDON
MIAMI RIO DE JANEIRO DELHI

ISBN 0 75411 552 6

First Published 2001 by
MINERVA PRESS
315–317 Regent Street
London W1B 2HS

Printed in Great Britain for Minerva Press

ANOTHER ANGEL

Acknowledgements

I would like to express my thanks to those people who have given me help and support in the completion of this book, in particular Dr Sarah Mohay-Ud-Din for her advice on medical matters, and Emma Apted and Claire Eaglestone for their comments and criticisms. I am especially grateful to Jason Browne for his constant encouragement and belief in me, and to my husband, Mike, for everything.

Contents

Going Home

I stare out of the taxi window. Sun-drenched roads and bright green grasses glide past. I squint as we turn into the sun. At last the station looms up into my field of vision. I have managed to avoid it for the entire length of my stay. At first I didn't want to see it because I thought it might be too tempting to launch myself on to a train home and ruin everything. When I left the station for the hotel, I told myself, 'The next time you see this station you will be going home.' Later, when my feelings about 'home' had become more mixed and complicated, I didn't want to see the launch pad that would take me back there. I preferred to ignore the pushing throng of time, going too quickly, too slowly, too madly. I wanted to forget that there was such a place, to be myself, whoever that was. Even now, I feel some ambivalence towards it. I have anticipated this moment a million times since my arrival, in many different shapes, forms and colours. Now that I am here, I realise it is none of them and all of them.

The day I arrived, I stepped off the train and took a glum bus ride to the hotel. It was pouring with rain, and strands of cold wove themselves around my nose and my fingertips. It was August. I squinted blithely at the road signs, trying to decipher them through the raindrops that uniformly coated the window. The simplicity of that difficulty; I would willingly return. I missed him then and the missingness took over my whole being, made me into a woman who was missing Joe and little else. I thought these two months would never be in the past. Now they are, all but the final trip home and yet I do not know whether they will ever really be gone.

An event is a strange entity, something that looks different from every angle. Its dimensions are uncountable and it is unrecognisable as the same object from all its different aspects. I sometimes wonder if we humans perceive shapes and colours in the same way: is my yellow a blue to someone else? I suppose we

7

will never know, since while we can put names to colours and communicate these names, the experience of a colour is qualitative and cannot be so captured.

I am going home, miraculously, home to Durham, to Joe, at last. I step out of the taxi into the glorious sunlight and allow myself a little smile. Anticipated moments are always welcomed, even when the emotion is closer to dread than to excitement. By the very act of pre-living them in our minds, we tie ourselves to them by a cord, a tight cord which stretches us towards them. The pressure is not loosened until the time arrives and we can press our bodies gloriously against the moment, feel its arms wrap around us, live in it, at last.

Is it the yellow aura of sunshine that makes Penzance Station a nicer place to be now? Is it possible that it is instead the glow of going-homeness, the idea of returning to Joe and to the life that I left suspended in Durham, the pause button pressed, the static buzzing away in my ear? The last time I was here, this populous station was the final destination on a long, gloomy train ride away from him. At least, I thought it was a destination; now I am undecided. Like events, destinations lose their sense of identity at the slightest push.

I shuffle on to the platform like an automaton and check the departures screen. The green letters are there, as formed as they always are, but the information does not quite reach my consciousness. My mind is full of Joe, of pictures of the new house that I have not yet lived in. Full of the flux that I have swum through in the preceding weeks and that I am relieved to have finally climbed out from. I know that I spent too long in the silvery liquid, now gliding, now flailing; but what choice did I have? The glittering pool was my life. The banks were steep but at the pre-appointed time I found a slope which I had no choice but to sliver myself up and then I wrapped myself in the comforting towels of home time. But have I really climbed out? Am I just on a ledge at low tide? I step out on to the platform, springfooted, barely noticing that my suitcase is heavy and my shoulders tired. I feel happy.

Despite everything, I am looking forward to being home. I have never been fond of journeys. I prefer to get them over with and wallow in my stationariness, my inertia, until such time as I am forced to take once more to my feet, or perhaps to my wings, and undertake another stage of movement. I suppose we never stop travelling in some small sense but mostly our journeys take us round and round in circles, or in some crazy variation of a circle, a two-dimensional shape that is too irregular to have a name. Two-dimensional; how to break out into a third? But it is the long-distance trips that really sour my heart.

I recoil slightly at the recollection of boarding the sludgy train in floods of tears all those weeks ago. I reach into my mind to find a picture of the woman that I am now, but all I find is one of a much younger Angel. She is just a sixth of a year younger than me but I cannot identify myself with her. I pity her; she has so much in front of her, so much to wade through before she reaches the bright, dry sunshine of now, so much more than she can know. She thinks it is simply a case of sitting it out and trying to bear being apart from Joe. She has only lately been in his arms, and I cannot help summoning up the image of their parting.

'Angel... I'm going to miss you so much.'

'Me too.' I sniffed a little but didn't let myself cry just yet. He held me tightly, clingingly, loath to release me. We kissed a melancholy, shaky kiss as the warm, late-summer air became tinged with the crisp starkness of winter. Joe too fought back the tears. Finally, he wrenched himself away from me to stand back on the cold, grey platform. His eyes, glistening with tears yet to fall, were glued to the receding train. I could see his desperation and aloneness mirroring my own.

Then, suddenly, I was trapped inside the carriage. I was hatching impossible plans to fight my way out, to somehow slip my body through the metal as it fled with me in its belly along the tracks. But it was impenetrable. The glass was toughened; the small squares of window that opened were too small to squeeze out of, the atoms of the metal and plastic were too tightly packed to swim between. I could be with Joe only by reversing time or the train. The first I did not profess to be able to do. The second I could perhaps manage with an enormous effort and an influx of strength but it would cause us great misery. There would be no job, no course, no money. I would have to go skulking with my tail between my legs back to London, back to my parents, back once again to my childhood, erasing everything I had been and achieved since the last time. I had been moving in these big circles for many years now, always ending up where I started and I was determined that it would not happen this time. But I could not think how I would bear the separation from Joe.

How is it that these pictures have the colour of something other than memories, something less and yet also something much more? I cannot be that Angel. She is too different from me, she is too past, too young, too happy, although she doesn't realise these things. What is she made up of? What am I made up of? Can it really be the same things when we are so unlike each other? I would like to meet her and warn her... but of what? Nothing I can do can prevent her from the emotional wrangles of the coming weeks. I feel useless, and can only look on from my safer position in the future.

When I am through this, will I look back and see the Angel that I am now as young, inexperienced? Will there be a chain of me stretching into the future, and into the past also, each seeing the previous but not the next? Would it help if we could, by some collective effort, turn our heads forward and see our futures?

A faint hum comes along the tracks, followed by some swirly wind and finally my train. It is packed with people who remind me of sausages, crammed inside the carriages, faces poking out of the cellophane packaging windows. A Lincolnshire, a Welsh pork-and-leek, some chipolatas, the odd salami, but mostly frozen, reconstituted pork-and-beefs. I am still at a loss as to how the time has passed. It has been slow for many different reasons, but still, consistently slow. Now it is ending, and in only hours' time I will feel Joe's strong arms folding me into his body, his lips renewing on mine the delicious sensation of kiss, his eyes confirming the loving words he will speak to me. And how will I take them? How will I respond to them? I wish I could prepare answers to throw at him but I have no idea what they should be.

The numbers on a clock face are arranged in a circle. We can forget the big hand for now, as its purpose is merely accuracy; it is the little hand that sweeps around the clock once every twelve hours. The largest number is twelve, and when the hour hand reaches this number it continues past and begins to move towards one again. Is the chain of Angels like this? When I reach my highest number, will I simply begin again? The numbers on a clock are always visible; it is only four o'clock at four o'clock because that is where the little hand happens to be. Is there a hand on my present, moving regularly forward, making me think that my life is linear, when really, if I knew how, I could take hold of the hand and point it at a different number?

Or am I a row of dominoes? A row of dominoes, each one falling prostrate, lifeless, when the moment it represents is past, passing the baton of Nowness to the next? If I am, then I cannot go back, only forward. Even if the dominoes are arranged in a circle, the process cannot begin again because the first domino will already have fallen. When I reach the last one, it will have nothing to pass my life on to and I will be a trail of fallen dominoes. My life broken, scattered in black and white over the obstacle course it followed while it still had life.

The motion of the train is lullaby-like. *Sweesh-swoosh, sweesh-swoosh.* I am tired and worn enough to give way to the rocking movement of the triangle-patterned seat beneath me. I lose myself in a sleepy reverie, in which I find Joe, smiling, kissing, loving me. He is there, tangibly there, and I can smell him, taste him, feel the texture of his skin, and I am with him. Weeks ago I tried in vain to will myself to this moment, to be only hours away from the end of our separation; I thought that once I was here, *here*, it would be ended. Now that I am, the few little hours seem still an eternity.

I vaguely dismiss my abysmal attempt to formulate some mathematical expression for this phenomenon, and unwillingly, yet with a hint of consent, proceed back into that future moment. I am pulled into his consciousness, he into mine. We pour ourselves each into the other's neck, unstopped bottles, uncorked at last, the heavy constraint of previous weeks giving way to the liquid of this new togetherness – this new, permanent togetherness.

A watched kettle never boils; and every detail of this particular kettle has been scrutinised right from the flicking of the switch. I listen for the faint thunder of the bubbling water, and, excited, catch a stomach-punching pre-echo from that long-awaited moment. I don't know any longer what the moment will be like. I don't think I really ever knew; I only thought I did. I don't feel that light-headed, pure joy that I used to feel in forecasting it, yet I know that I cannot wait to see the steam pouring out of the spout, the second click as the kettle switches itself off. Occasionally I wonder whether this has all been a bizarre concoction of my imagination. The last few weeks have been so different to and so disjointed from everything else in my life that I have sometimes felt the Everything Else to be a delusion. I have disjointed myself from my past before – I am an old hand at that – but never from the future at the same time in this way.

Close to boiling, like the kettle, I slide off my jumper. The heat is flowing out from the little vents by my feet and whirling and whorling around the train. If I put my foot on the heater, the hotness creeps up my ankle and then my leg, leaving invisible beads of itchy sweat where it has crawled. I can open the windows but still I feel the artificial heat searing at me.

Heating and air-conditioning systems; generating summer when it is winter, winter when it is summer, neither in particular when it is spring or autumn. They turn heat to cold and cold to heat just as they are expected to. People dress for the weather but the artificial weather systems are always there to foil them. In the hot, blissful days of summer, the sun beats down upon the outdoors-goer, the heat haze skirts every road, every pavement, the fumes from traffic have no room to cool down before they hit the faces of pedestrians, and little fires seem to burn in the air. We look at the wilting flowers, the yellowing grass, the wilting and yellowing humans around us, and all of us – shoppers, train travellers, restaurant-goers – know by instinct that we must wear as little as possible. We deck ourselves in flimsy material, we bare our white, wilting bodies, we move slowly and heat-exhaustedly towards our ever-changing destinations.

Meanwhile, in the trains, in the restaurants, the air conditioning blows out bits of Antarctica, snowy rushes of air for the tips of our noses, sleeves of ice for our bare arms. We enter them and freeze. Until the winter, when, wrapped in our soft wool jumpers, enormous coats and floppy hats, we swarm into tropical supermarkets and Augustian department stores, sweating and sweltering, half-wishing for the summer and the cold, breezy air to cool us. Modernity seems to have confused, if not reversed, the roles of the seasons. Summer is hardly summer when you have to carry a thick coat with you so that you can go shopping. Something of the heat, the sunlight, the doziness of those thick afternoons is lost.

I turn to the window of the train and a flurry of colours dances into my consciousness. In the summer, when the days were warmer, I was cold and I shivered, my world was filled with the sights and sounds of freezing blues and greys. And yet now, as my train hurtles towards the place my heart has never really left and yet no longer truly belongs, it is winter. My life is becoming a warm orange, ever warmer, until eventually I will fall into the blisteringly hot arms of my lover. I cannot seem to identify the colours of the intervening weeks. Perhaps there were at first ever deeper blues, and towards the end, mustard-yellows. In between, I think purples and greens... mad colours, crazy colours, unknown colours, as everything I knew darted out of my control and out of my comprehension.

Out of the window, I only half-see the trees that go from being in front to behind with a sudden lurch. They loom big and proud ahead, large-scale and impressive, and then, seconds later, they are gone, forgotten; it is as if they had not existed. When I was very young, I sometimes travelled on trains and looked at the trees. I always felt that they were crowding behind me, following the train in a silent conspiracy. Afterwards, I played an obscure game with my brothers – a game where they were the trees and I the train, and they crept behind me, as if unseen, arm-branches waving as they attempted to emulate the sinister creaking sound of an old oak in the wind. My task would be to swing around as suddenly as I could and catch them in the act of walking, but each time I twisted to face them it was only their arms that were waving with a soft rustle in the wind.

They always laughed, and I, their younger sister, could only emulate them; but for me, the laughter had been forced, a thin veil covering my real and deep fear that one morning I would wake to find the trees, a multitude of old, diseased and angry trees, crowding around my bed, creaking and cracking relentlessly at me as I screamed and rocked back and forth in terror.

My nightmares as a child were always vivid and terrifying. There were always trees and I was always overwhelmed and suffocated by them. The wind blew, and it was dark, leaves sweeping up from the forest floor in the gusts. I would be lost there, my feet endlessly padding the soft carpet of leaves. There were often canopies of leaves and branches above my head, completing my encasement – trees all around, above, and even underfoot. Sometimes I would look up through the branches at the stars, and all would become silent, still, benign, but then the stars themselves would begin to arch down at me, falling, propelling, down, down, and the world would start to spin, until I had to look away from them, back at the old, old trees.

There was never any well-defined threat. I never ran from or trembled at anything specific. But I always ran and I always trembled. There were sometimes bits of roots that sprang out of the ground to trip me, or tendrils that plaited themselves into my hair and pulled me back towards I don't know what. Sometimes there were people, to whom I would reach out as I ran, whom I knew could pluck me out of the nightmare and toss me safely back into my own mattress, pillows and duvet. But they would be unable to reach me, or, worse, they would merely laugh at me, laugh at my terror and my distress. Quite often these people were my brothers.

Eventually I grew up, and the nightmares didn't trouble me for many years; I even forgot about them. But since my dream on that dark, catastrophic night in the hotel, they have been creeping constantly and endlessly back into my consciousness. I was alone that night; I had not been the previous night, and as I awoke with no one beside me and in a sweaty terror the disaster was brought home to me doubly. I should have realised that I was going to dream, should have prepared myself for it, but there was hardly room in my head for another thought when I lowered it on to the soft pillow that was invisibly stained with the sleepy excretions of someone else, now gone.

I was feeling fragile and lonely. I have always felt fragile but I had been reminded just how tentative happiness is and just how delicate even the strongest of us really are. I suppose I am the same person as that other, younger Angel because we share the same body, even if mine is imperceptibly more aged; yet how can a person consist of something that is so fragile that it can fall into dust at any moment? Our bodies, the lesser part of us, may be the same but our minds certainly are not. There are traces of the same thoughts, similar memories – or at least memories of similar events – and we have sprung through life together, droplets from the same fountain. She is my twin, not myself.

I blink Bryony out of my eyes, and through my lowered eyelids I look out of the window. There are fields with distant motorways running through them and occasionally some tiny houses. The sky is the only constant thing as the landscapes fly past, a million different postcard scenes, a million people's lives flashing past; unseen, unintimated. Then the town begins to draw near and we rattle past a row of houses very like the one that I was brought up in. Edwardian, terraced, some of these houses display proud extensions or loft conversions that scramble over their tangled gardens anachronistically. No doubt they improve the living accommodation and resale value of each individual house, but to the whole they lend only an untidy, shambling appearance.

The train is slowing down on its approach to the station. This is when the modern train sounds most like a steam engine; we have not really come that far, after all. We travel faster and perhaps further in these modern times but the mechanism is essentially the same. I look out on to gardens, long and thin, many of them containing a shed or two – broken-down, corrugated iron roofs battered and flimsy. A greenhouse sometimes rears up, and if I look really hard I think I can see the tomato plants inside, mostly bereft of their fruit now, having gone from green to red-green back to almost green alone. Children are playing in one of these gardens, trampling the vegetable patch, ducking and hiding from each other behind the protruding jagged edges of the house, under bushes, behind trees.

The train is now stationary. A little girl wanders away from the others and stoops to pick a late daisy or a piece of clover. The others are still playing in a boisterous group, but I suppose *she* is tired of whatever games they are immersed in. She remains crouched on the floor, her young face resplendent with concentration, and I wonder what it is that has captured her attention. Her hair is long and straight and flows down her back, mostly neatly and squarely, although around her face it shoots out in the crazy directions of a playful child's tumbling hair. She is scrutinising something in the utmost detail.

★

A small girl discovers a cat in her sprawling London garden. Tiny and afraid, little bigger than a kitten, it crouches behind a comforting lavender bush. Mewing with hunger and loneliness, it demands attention, and yet shies away from the girl in fear. Carefully, patiently, she coaxes it out from its hiding place. She presents before it a saucer of milk. Friendless and with no choice but to place its trust in the kind little girl, it clings to her. It follows her around the garden, mewing ever more loudly, sometimes venturing to paw at her hair. It is summer, and the sun is hot. It throws dark shadows over the garden in patches so that she will always know where the trees are without looking at them. Sometimes a wispy cloud makes the shadows melt into the grass, and she waits, full of tension, for them to come back.

★

I wonder about the nature of memory; it has always intrigued me. It often seems that we are the person our past makes us, and indeed my psychology lectures have confirmed this view. Sometimes the tiny details of our past can be relevant to the present, can even have formed our present in its entirety. Sometimes we try to cleanse our minds of the little black spots that impede our vision of the future but which will not come out. Lady Macbeth's stains were only visible in her head, and these small blots have a similar existence. I suppose that at some point in my future these weeks I have spent in Penzance will be a tiny blot somewhere in the back of my mind, but whether or not I continue to be beset by the events themselves, I know that they have left indelible trails in my head that no amount of scrubbing will remove.

Going There

Beethoven. Dull-rough and Classical, shining with tradition and progress. Stormily Romantic, wildly passionate, the innovative, Promethean master. Those who came after him fell into the great, dark shadow of his opus, his gargantuan work, toiled beneath the impression of his mighty shoulder. The apotheosis of Classicism, the dawn of Romanticism, the incorporation of everything, not only past and present, but future also.

I heave my luggage off the train and on to the platform, and for some reason I smile. The first leg of my journey has gone smoothly; or at least, the first leg of this part of my journey, for it is really a portion of a much larger one. I glance around, almost expecting to see Joe there to meet me; a ludicrous thought. The station looks different in this direction. The winter sunshine is forcing its way in through the decaying rafters and there is no sign of the miserable drizzle that beset my spirits on that vague but intense August day.

There is an uncanny symmetry to this journey, or set of journeys. First, there is the obvious layer; I am following the same route home, only in reverse. The stations that were at the end of my trip to Penzance are at the beginning of my trip home – this is true of all return journeys. But there is more to it than that. As I sat here on this dismal station that Other Time, I was missing Joe. Now I am missing Joe. As time passed away in Penzance, I felt all kinds of other emotions, but now, I have come back to missing Joe. I was frightened, sad and confused on that other journey, and I am confused, sad and frightened now; but in between I felt many other things. The whole experience has been somewhat cyclical. I had more return tickets than I thought.

There is some time before my connection, so I drag my leather and plastic companions and myself to a small bench by the side of the railway line. I peer into the shadows, and I can almost see the Angel that sat on this station waiting to depart for

Penzance. That Angel – this Angel, although the connection is hard to believe – struggled towards the train, contemplating failing to board, yet knowing that she must, finally installing herself in a corner for the last part of her sad journey.

Corners have always seemed so much more secure to me. So much more shelter from the biting wind, which had somehow accompanied me into the carriage and was buffeting my insides, despite the clement weather outdoors. I had formed my own clouds inside my body, my own gusts of icy wind, my own sharp, stinging rain. The squirrels and rabbits and foxes had run for cover, for shelter, had started burrowing and scratching at the foothills and treescapes of my body. I could not shelter because I *was* the world. My own little ecosystem was thrashing at me, wanting to destroy me.

I tried to keep my distance from the strangers around me. They made a mockery of my doleful countenance; children on a seaside trip, businessmen who would be back with their loved ones this evening, travellers with backpacks and flasks of warm coffee. I heard only sinister snatches of their conversations, each component from a different mouth, a different group. The low rumble of the train served as the horror music, underpinning the banal, as in all the best thriller movies. I tried to turn down the receptivity of my ears, and glanced out of the window at the rain-sodden homes that hugged the railway line, as if for security, in much the same way that I cosseted myself up in this corner of the carriage. I stared at the mournful, grey sky.

Two hours to Paddington from here. I will settle down to watch the sunshine-ridden world turn from one populated by bustling buildings and organised greenery to the impressive sprawl of the countryside, punctuated sparingly with habitations of varying sizes. Then nature will once more give way to nurture, gradually, almost imperceptibly at first, but gathering speed as that of the train decreases, until I will find myself among the tower blocks and the iron railings of London.

The mad dash across the underground is my least favourite part of the journey. I think of cigarettes: the smell of fresh smoke and of stale ash. Both come into the underground as ghosts on the breaths of the sorry people who are not allowed to smoke once beneath the city – each as bad as the other. The chocolate machines on the platforms look as old and worn as the people who whitely and tirelessly fly through the corridors each day. The people are always different in London: the adventurous capital somehow seems to steal the spirit of its inhabitants for itself, to turn them into mere parts of the huge, bristling machine, and to switch off the brightness from their eyes. London is a ghost town, full of live yet haunted people who would not belong anywhere else on the planet.

And then King's Cross. The litter here whirls as effortlessly out of the tunnels as the people with whom it shares its passage: crumpled crisp packets; flattened boxes that used to contain cigarettes; chocolate wrappers and fast food drinks cartons. The smells of burgers and salads mix in the air, giving contradictory nutritional messages to the olfactory sensors of those who are not too accustomed to notice any more. The huge forecourt looms over the lives of a thousand people as they spend varying fractions of their lives getting somewhere, getting nowhere, ending up just where they began.

The train to Darlington will be full of commuters to begin with. Moustaches, suits, laptop computers sprawled across the tables and raincoats rolled up in accomplished balls beside them. They don't have the bowler hats these days but they don't need them; evolution has left the impression of them on the heads and faces of these constant travellers. But how disheartening, surely, to travel, always travel, but never find anywhere new? To get on the same train each day and move backwards and forwards, up and down the same straight stretch of track, covering the same grey stretch of ground day after day.

Perhaps they look so grey and suffocated because they rarely get their heads out above the surface of London other than to bury them in the grey tower buildings, or to lay them on their plush but grey pillows at night. If I was a commuter, I would work in a different office every day. I would want my journey to be a worthwhile one, to get somewhere, rather than to travel again and again in the same sorry circles.

Then, as London becomes an increasingly distant memory, the work-worn wayfarers will fall through the filter and leave only the long-distance runners, restless and sleepy, watching the sun fall slowly down through the sky. They look out of the windows, unlike the commuters who have seen it all before and do not realise that it is constantly changing. They look out at the landscapes, skies, towns, villages and farms, but even they think, This is what this journey looks like. They too would not recognise it on a different day.

Peterborough will flit past, as though I had never lived there, as though I had never slept there at night while my life fell about my ears in the darkness. It will not recognise me. The towers of the cathedral will not bend towards me, arms to welcome me back. The river will not leap out of its ditch to shake my hand. There will be no fanfare of bugles on the station platform. Then Darlington Station will be empty in the evening; a different place entirely to the bustle of that August morning when I jostled with the faceless commuters for seats on the train. And then, the last train, home to Durham, to the sleepy station nestled in the hillside, the quiet, dewy mornings. Home.

If my weeks in Penzance were part of the same journey, at what point did I turn around and begin the return portion? Which temporal-emotional destination was the terminus? Which were merely intermediate platforms? Why was I not provided with a timetable, a map? Why could I not have taken a different route?

My tears fell like smeary raindrops on to my lap. On the platform, Joe was shrinking before my eyes, already too small for me to read his facial expression. Soon the colours of his hair, face and clothes merged, and he was a crudely painted toy soldier, his movements now too small for recognition. Eventually he was just a blob, and then he became swallowed up by the platform, which itself began to lose its features, faster and faster now as the train gathered speed. By the time the station disappeared into the perspective marks I could have drawn on the page of my field of vision, the tears were beginning to subside, through a massive effort of restraint.

I concentrated hard on the sound of the train moving along the tracks, the *clickety-click* of childhood, feeling its rhythms, knowing by it when the train changed its speed. I wanted the racket to drown out my thoughts, my despair, but instead it began to serve as a reminder of my desperation: *clickety-click*, away from him, *clickety-click*, faster and faster, away from him, *away* from him, *away from him*. It mocked my senses, until I closed my eyes and made a concerted effort to mask it out.

Music can take hold of our existence, borrow it for the duration and then return it, unharmed, although possibly altered, when it is over. This is one of the things I like about music. It can entangle itself in our brains, run through our blood, fill our veins full to bursting, and no damage is done. There are other things that can infiltrate our fragile bodies with less benign results. Music has infinite power over human sensibilities, yet we can choose when to let it command us.

I have lived in my new home for almost two months now, but I have spent a total of about half an hour inside the house. I wonder if I have rosied my images of it during my time away, but then I remember my excitement on finding it, and I am certain that it is as perfect as I see it in my mind. It is a small house, with few but large rooms. The front door is presented in the frame of an enormous arched porch, of the kind that I always dreamed of having nestling at the entrance to my house; arms outstretched to provide a shelter from the outside world, it makes the lines of the house less angular and more sweeping.

The bay window stands proudly to the left of the porch, and when the weather is cold and the lights of the house are orange and warming, the people outside in the drizzle will look enviously in. A chimney stack gives outsiders evidence of the open fireplaces that hug the walls inside. They remind me of stories I read as a child, and I picture little boys and girls in smocks and bonnets rustling through the rooms of the house. If such people had existed, they would be old men and women by now, or perhaps they would be dead. I am never quite sure of when the things we see in history ended and the world as it is today began, and I suppose I have a romantic view of anything that happened before around thirty years prior to my birth. This is undoubtedly unrealistic but I prefer to keep it intact. What is the use of science if it makes us less happy?

Back in the sloping stillness of Durham, where the rain

trickles down the hills and collects in great puddles at the lowest points, is home. The house stands proudly and individually at the end of its row; it is the only one like it in the street. I see it as caught between the last two centuries, an idea which has tremendous appeal to me; a piece of chronological reality amongst crazy surroundings. The bricks are rough to the touch, and the wide, wooden window frames are painted a thick, glossy white. I am only disappointed that it is not of an age to have a cellar. The garden path curls around the house like a moat on three sides, and at the back of the house it leads to a largely neglected garden. At the end of this garden there is a wooden shed, rather like the one at the house I grew up in. I have pretty ideas of putting this to all sorts of interesting uses, although in the back of my mind I know it will be full of boxes and lawnmowers and old, unwanted furniture before very much time can pass.

When I first saw Durham it was heavy with snow. Joe took me there in the January of my final year at Nottingham, just when the rush and chaos of Christmas was over and the new year was too young to have had any effect as yet. The bare branches of the trees were bent almost to the ground by the weight of the snow. Wherever people went they left their tracks, printed indelibly, until the thaw at least (because nothing is really for ever), in the sprinkly covering. They sludged around in their fur-lined boots, the few lone people who ventured out; the town seemed empty, as the majority of the students had not yet come back from their cosy Christmas holidays. The world was white and fluffy with cold, but we basked in the warmth of being together.

'What do you think then?' Joe had asked with the pride of a father displaying a favourite son in a plush-lined glass display cabinet.

'It's a wonderful town,' I said, smiling back shyly. We had still been together for only a little time and I was feeling overwhelmed by his company. I meant it when I told him I was impressed with his beloved home town, but I think that at the time I loved it as much for being his, for being an extension of Joe, as for its own qualities.

A snowball rushed past my head, close enough to frighten me

but at a sufficiently ludicrous trajectory that I knew it had not been intended to hit me. 'Hey!' I mock-screamed. I started to scoop up the cold snow in my bare hands, tried not to grimace at the icy snakes that began to thread themselves into my veins, and rustled together a rather square weapon.

'Oh no, you don't!' he commanded, running towards me. In his attempts to grab the snowball from me, he slid his foot across the snow-covered surface and we both fell to the ground, cushioned by its temporary softness, laughing. Then, there was the unmistakable taste and sensation of kiss, and his limbs pressing against my body, and I was insensible to the cold.

'Anyway, just as well you like it, since you'll be living here soon.' He was grinning, but there was a serious glaze beneath the rough, lumpy facade. I was shocked at the broaching of this idea so early in our relationship, yet at the same time I felt almost suffocated by the warm glow that the image produced in my throat.

I have been to Durham so many times since, that I remember little about that first weekend, but I do know that my first impressions of the town have not changed much. We walked down a slippery hill into the rambling shops, past colleges that seemed to me more charming and less grandiose than those of Cambridge or Oxford, where I had always felt inferior and unwelcome. Durham seemed to hold its hilly arms open to me, and I was loath to return to big, grimy Nottingham. As we walked through the circular streets of the town, Joe's arm was around my waist, the white, gleaming Christmas air was still rife around us, and I relaxed into snug happiness.

★

The cat has become very fond of the child and clings to her legs. It is brightly tortoiseshell, and the markings that cover it intrigue the little girl. The fur is soft and four little paws sport tiny claws which the growing cat would not dream of using to hurt anyone. Every day it waits for her to get home from school, and it never accepts attention from anyone but her. Secretly, she feels smug; how delicious to have a creature totally dependent upon her, that relies upon her for its every comfort, its every necessity. Her brothers resent this monopoly, and although she tries to make it play with them, nothing she can do induces it to trust anyone but her. She is its saviour, its mother, its heroine, its icon.

★

Sometimes when I wake from sleep, I flounder after dreams that are instantly purged of all but a few impossibly coloured details. I struggle to pull their meaning out of the mist, to form some kind of sense from the nonsensical images that I am left with, but usually this is to no avail. In the past I have cursed such dreams, but I would have welcomed them in these last few weeks. It is worse to wake suddenly with your body swathed in sweat and your limbs sticky with fear, to know every element of the horrific dream that has just racked your sleep. Every minute detail, every last pounding of your heart is as vivid and as real as the sheets that cradle you and the air that seems to be rushing into your parched throat.

My eye is caught by a slender young woman with flowing brown hair. There is a woolly knocking at my stomach and my legs brace themselves automatically to approach her; but she is a stranger. I sigh, suddenly recognising the futility of my attempts to remove Bryony from my thoughts. Anticipation of Durham and of Joe, the end of the course, the logistics of my movements towards home; none of it is enough. I am foolish to attempt forgetfulness so soon. A woman like Bryony is not easily removed from one's consciousness. Bryony: young, attractive, quietly confident, unusually intelligent. I was captivated by her. I failed to see how anyone could resist Bryony's grasp and charm. Bryony: unique and irresistible, breathing a comforting fire over my icy cold body.

★

The cat curls up in the child's arms. She strokes it tenderly and thinks about getting up to give it milk, but it looks so comfortable that she does not. All is peaceful in the room. Dolls and toy cars are lying strewn over the floor, but they are no longer a subject of interest. Two young faces appear in the room, carried by their strong, agile legs and feet. Marcus is eleven and his brother, Daniel, is nine. They stroke the cat, but it mews at the girl and paws itself deeper into her lap. She reproaches them, as a six-year-old might be expected to express displeasure at two older brothers in a conspiracy, and they begin to taunt her. They grasp at the cat, and she draws it still further into her.

Marcus and Daniel exchange glances, and then, adeptly, the elder brother reaches out and pulls the cat from her grasp. Their sister bursts instantly into tears and wails at them, but they run off, giggling in their childish, high-pitched tones. For a moment she stands on the spot, in her knee-length dress bespeckled with flowers and her little red buckle-up shoes, and the tears pour out of her like raindrops from a burst cumulus. Then she takes up the chase. Her brothers make exclamations of glee as they carry the frightened bundle out of the door at the back of the house. They run slowly at first, and she begins to brighten as she feels she will catch them, but, a cruel tease, their legs accelerate when she gets near. She wants to cover her ears to shut out the distressed cries of her cat, but does not because she knows that this will impair her efforts to run. The boys dart around the side of the house. Their sister follows them, but when she reaches the corner bricks, her eyes scan around and she cannot locate them. The sobs begin again, and she blindly takes a direction, which may or may not be the right one; she will never know, because she does not find them.

★

How do I know what is real? If an event did happen, is it still real if I can't remember it? Is it real now, emerging out of a dark cloud of unreality, just because I have remembered it? And conversely, does it matter that it never happened if I believe it did? If we are made up from our memories, are we real when our memories are false? How do I know if I am a real person? How do I know what is real?

History is full of things that aren't real, for a number of reasons. Sometimes the truth was covered up as the event unfolded, as knowledge of it would have changed the course of history in a manner unamiable to its perpetrators. Sometimes historians put together scanty pieces of evidence, genuinely, honestly, but they end up, quite unwittingly, with the wrong picture. Sometimes history is changed into something we would like better. But once the story is changed, officially, definitively, which narrative is correct?

A researcher uncovers definitive evidence that a royal marriage centuries ago never actually took place. Or, perhaps, that the son of a queen was not also the son of her husband. The researcher painstakingly traces the trail to the present day and identifies the 'real' monarch. Centuries of history invalidated. Monarchs faked, lesser aristocrats denied their 'true' right to rule. But what is the truth if the marriage papers were never really signed, if a certain queen at a certain time shared a bed with a certain man who was not the king?

The researcher now has two choices. Choice one: he reveals his discovery and throws the past up into a big mess above his head. What now? Is the monarch dethroned and the lucky winner of the crown thrust into Buckingham Palace? Is it decided that something that happened so long ago is irrelevant and therefore, by implication, no longer real? Or, choice two: he keeps his secret to himself, knowing that if he wrecks history he will no longer know who he is himself. The offending event was a lie but life since then has perhaps been real. What is one false event amongst an infinite number of true ones? Are the facts really always the truth?

I sigh impatiently at myself. The thick black hands of the station clock are too still and I wish I could will them around. The Roman numerals smile down nonchalantly at me, all but one, which is partially hidden behind the elaborate curls of the minute hand. I get up once more and stare down the track but there is no sign of any train. Even a train going somewhere else would be a comfort but I can see none. It is as though the station has died, or is suspended in some trainless place. A fantastical panic rises up inside me, a notion that the train will never come and the rest of the world will never miss me.

I reproach myself for these thoughts. They are the wild creations of a woman who wants to get home to her lover, to her new life, away from the past. I urgently need to put this recent past well away into the recesses of my mind, to begin to forget it. I know it will take a large amount of time and perhaps a larger amount of effort, and yet I am desperate to begin. And no less desperately, I want to see Joe. I have missed him, all through the turmoil of these weeks, despite everything, despite myself. I need to forget the agony, the battering my already fragile identity has taken, all the pain and all the doubts. I know I want to, I know that I want Joe and the life I have chosen. I have learnt much from my recent experiences. Although much of this new knowledge is conflicting and self-contradictory, I want things to be positive from now on. There is no question that I want to be with Joe; the only question there has ever been is whether or not I will let myself have what I want, the question that has been prominent in most of my life to this point.

The rude sound of computer-generated bells, and then the rasping voice of the bored station announcer informs me that my train is the next arrival on platform two. I make my customary last-minute check through my pockets to ensure that none of my belongings have taken the opportunity to make their escape. Then I step up on to the train, my suitcase companions wagging their leathery tails behind them.

Arrival

It is still difficult to believe the manner in which I was whisked away from my impending comfortable life and into the bowels of Penzance. When I received the letter, I felt as though my world was about to end. I had been longing for this job – in fact, I had been relying on getting it; it was to some extent my last chance. My degree was finally over – I had managed to last out a full three years without giving up – and now all I wanted to do was get out into the world and practise my counselling on real people. Real people, in real trouble, not paper, textbook characters or students pretending to be patients. The interview round was tough, and I cannot remember the number of rejections I received. I was actually beginning to feel that the whole three years had been a waste of time, that I would have been better off trudging to Peterborough market three days a week, standing in the voluptuous air and calling out mindless facts about the price of pineapples day in and day out.

The market stall had in fact been more of a challenge than I had anticipated. I started work there just as I began to emerge from my dreadful, exhausting depression. I was nervous but I had thought my problems would have been boredom and excessive melancholy rather than any difficulty with the work itself. My lungs were never quite up to the standards required and I was invariably hoarse at the end of the day. As the hours ticked by, the smell of rotten fruit would germinate, gradually climbing up through my nose and playing havoc inside my sinuses, until sometimes I could feel the particles in there, the tunnels in my head like a water park to those outrageous airborne creatures.

I stare out of the window at the last vestiges of Devon. A place of moors and rainy, windy days, a place to fly kites in the gloom, a place of sunny cream-tea picnics in summer fields. It feels wrong to be merely passing through. The faint hills ramble past, the train rumbles over them. Soon Somerset will be upon me, but I do not know exactly when. Aeroplanes often have complex-looking navigation systems that enable their passengers to keep a track of where they are. I am sceptical as to the accuracy of these systems; sometimes I feel sure that they proceed at a pre-programmed rate and follow a set course, regardless of whether the bright, cold wings carry the great chunks of metal as planned, and yet it is nevertheless comforting to have some sense of orientation.

Trains are not like that. There are no signs as you would find along a road. Every now and then, if I strain out of the window, I can spy one, but it never tells me where I am. If I am lucky, I might see a road number, or find out in which direction a major town or a village I have never heard of lies, but I am never any the wiser as to my actual position. I am trapped, carried inevitably along by the pristine machinery that scorns geography. A track is a track is a track. The stations are the only points of distinction, and a journey consists of giving oneself up to the random passage of the time between these stations. Once on the train, distance seems to disappear from the equation. A landmark or two may pop out but they are always at the wrong angles, in the wrong places, their relationships with each other distorted.

I remember taking a train from Portsmouth to Waterloo when I was a child. Somewhere in the vicinity of Vauxhall I saw Big Ben looming between the high-rise flats, sometimes partially hidden behind strings of drying tea towels. I remember my horror at the association of something so grand with the poverty and despair I could sense by the railway lines even at that age. Rail travel is a perversion of reality.

It was, of course, always only a matter of time before I dragged myself back, back to the academic showcase, the thick, heavy environment of learning and stale enthusiasm. I had left two degrees behind: one of them before it had even started, the other after I had reached the halfway point. I suppose I had always known that I would go back and get those elusive letters after my name sooner or later, but I had never imagined studying counsel-ling. It was a quirk in my own fate that finally drove me to this course of study. In the past I had always done what I wanted to, thought of myself before the other people in my or any other universe. It was by chance that I decided to volunteer as a Samaritan. Several days a week at the market stall was not an adequate use of my time, and I would find myself on my days off wandering around markets in neighbouring towns, just to taste that fruit-ridden air, to listen to the mingling cries of the vendors, to be annoyed by the bustle of the whole market square. And then the Samaritans' advert caught my eye.

I suppose I felt that, as well as helping others, I could find something of use to myself. I had come through the worst of the depression, simply by paying my rent and sitting inside my four walls, by living through it, but I did not want to risk going through the rest alone. There came a point where I knew I had to take a step out of the quagmire or, far though I had come, I could quite easily fall back in and have to start the difficult climb out from scratch. And I knew the pain of loneliness and despair, I understood what it was to be confronted by an all-encompassing doom that could not be driven away. I thought I could use my knowledge and experience to help, and one thing that I really needed at this vital stage of my recovery was to feel useful, valued.

Bristol flies into view, arriving ever more slowly, until I feel that the train will never actually reach it but instead crawl ever on towards it, asymptotically. Some people start to gather their belongings together, and the delicate wire of stillness and travelling is broken, like the ping of a violin string.

I still marvel at the infinite number of problems the world was able to throw at me in those months. There are far more drunks, drug abusers and wife-beaters in the world than I had ever imagined. These people were frequent callers, so much so that I even came to know some of them and, unbelievably, think of them as friends by the time I left.

There were also the melancholy people; not depressed, too alive and vital to be depressives – or in any case, far more in touch with reality than I ever was in the depths of my gloomy pool of stagnation and unhappiness – but somehow disillusioned with life. Sometimes they had a concrete reason, but not always. Often they were simply struggling to find a meaning, and at times I found myself frustrated at my inability to provide them with one. The basic training I was given told me what answers to give, but I was always hollowly aware that they were inadequate. I am not sure how much good I threw out into the world, how much hope, if any – if such a thing can be quantified – I inspired, but I do know that my mentors were pleased with the way I undertook the work, and this made me more proud of myself than I had felt at any other time in my life.

I am not sure if it is true that I had an aptitude for the task, but it was the only thing I had managed to do remotely well thus far in my life, and I decided that I could make it my career. I entered the first year of my counselling degree with a pre-knowledge of many of the problems I would be studying, and an experience and insight that many of the staff lacked. My crises of confidence were few; I saw the course through and came out of it a fully fledged counsellor.

I was a graduate; after so many failed attempts, it felt like waking up in the morning from a series of bad dreams. And soon, I was a graduate with a job offer, something that not many of my contemporaries could claim to be. Then, some small amount of time after I accepted the job, my summons arrived in the post one morning. I was court-martialled; poisoned out of my newly blissful existence, my plans all spoiled, and Joe's too. An eight-week course in the middle of nowhere, hundreds of miles from where I wanted to be! It sent me reeling.

I felt I was still in one of the nightmares. I had known about the induction course, or at least that I was required to attend one, but had been given no further details. I told myself that eight weeks was not really all that long and that in the future it would seem to have passed in a twinkling of my newly qualified eyes, but somehow this failed to be of comfort to me. The date was pure poetry; suddenly I almost believed in fate and divine intervention. To expect me to travel to the far corner of the island on the day that Joe and I were committed to moving into our new house was preposterous; however, it was also real, and we both knew that there would be a solution, however unsatisfactory.

I was almost angry at Joe for having nothing to worry about but missing me, when I had the course itself to endure on top of being without him. It seemed exactly the type of event I had hoped to avoid, exactly the scenario that was often put forward by employers in the name of 'selection centres', which I had congratulated myself on missing. It was like a gruelling interview after the job offer. Reading through the agenda was like glancing through the script of one of my most grotesque imaginings. I was not able to rid myself of this script throughout the long journey to Penzance, and on arriving I clutched it tightly, a self-defence mechanism.

I constructed myself a kind of a litany: 'Everything I will experience is calculated to cause the greatest possible amount of embarrassment and distress. Everyone there will be feeling as bad as I will. I do not need to see any of the other people again if I choose not to.' I expected to choose not to; the thought of making friends at such a place as this was ludicrous. We were all there to grit our teeth and get through it – a kind of judgement day, where failure would almost certainly mean the end of a career before it had begun.

Human tragedy is something that we take for granted. It is impossible to realise this until such a tragedy strikes you. Until then, you hear about other people's misfortunes and you feel sorry for them but you have no sense of the impact that a death, an illness or even a job redundancy can have on a life, or on a number of lives. We are all so shut away inside our little cocoons that we let nothing impact on our plush, cosy surroundings. It is only when the trouble gets inside that we notice it. I suppose this is a good thing; we are bombarded with other people's tragedies throughout our lives, and we could not possibly react to each one. But when it finally strikes you, you need other people to feel with you, to experience with you, and they never do.

When I wandered into the oversized reception, my worst fears were realised. To some extent this was deliberate; I had spent so much time and energy being afraid of this moment that to prove myself wrong now would be almost a failure, a disappointment. I suppose what I mean is that had it not lived up to my worst fantasies, I would have convinced myself that it did. I had no need to pretend. I gulped. This is where I would be spending the next eight weeks, inside these gaudy walls, with a group of naive, chuckling people. I would fail. There was no alternative.

A fake cappuccino was thrust into my hand from somewhere,

and I fell into the plush, burgundy armchair, fat and ugly in its greedy rolls of material. Somewhere in the distance behind my eyes, tears were close to forming, and I wondered how I would prevent their existence. I bathed my lips in the smooth, creamy froth which threatened to scald them, and thought of Joe, his lips on mine, the stubble beneath his mouth pricking me deliciously, his soft, pale cheeks cushioning my own. Eight weeks. It was a sentence. No, a paragraph, I mused wryly. Pages and pages of my life were unfolding in the wrong place and with the wrong people, and there was nothing I could do to prevent this from happening.

In desperation, I pulled into focus the groups of people around me – for they had formed themselves into little cliquey bands already, and were eloquising fashionably with one another. They looked big, powerful, commanding, and I felt frightened. Then my eyes lifted as a kinder-looking woman entered the room. Her face was not set into the hefty plastic grin of the others and her movements were not as deliberate and methodical. Her clothes hung loosely on her deft body, fitting perfectly. The seat beside me was vacant and Bryony wafted into it. Neither of us spoke; coffee was of primary importance. Her hair was chestnut-brown and thin and wisped around the freckles on her face in little untidy rushes. Her skin looked smooth and pale but full of vitality and more alive and pulsing than any I had seen before. She was delicate, and looked different from any of the other women I had encountered at the hotel so far.

I tried to picture this stranger clothed in the corporate standard short skirt, black clinging tights and metallic-buttoned silk covering icy breasts. Deliberately engineered to provide the nimble-eyed with a taste of intricate yet necessarily robust underwear. It was as if these garments offered the perceptive an insight into their personalities, or at any rate those that they wished to display. Such attire did not fit the girl's image, and I felt glad that she had not sacrificed an obvious dislike for such garments. I looked down out of the corner of my eye at my own suit and felt a pang of distaste. Sighing inwardly, I turned my attention once more to my coffee, fearful that my neighbour might sense this unprovoked attention.

I have sometimes thought that I knew what was fundamental to life, what it was that made me and retained me in the form I am, that I had solved the puzzle of my own nature and origin. Each time I was wrong. Is knowledge circular? Aristotle thought that all matter was infinitely divisible, that you could keep on breaking things up into smaller and smaller components and never get to the smallest one. From Greek times, the atom was thought to be the most fundamental element, right up until the twentieth century, when protons, neutrons and electrons were discovered. These too are now known to be made up of quarks, and although scientists have identified theoretical limits as to how far this hierarchy can go, who knows whether or not it will go on for ever? Thus, Aristotle could be right after all. I don't think we will ever know. A generation may prove a scientific fact beyond doubt, only for it to be overturned by means of a stunning piece of lateral thinking from the next.

My thought processes sometimes work like this. You think you have found the flash of inspiration, that you know the answer, and yet tomorrow your solution will be impossible. Quarks come in six flavours: up, down, strange, charmed, top and bottom; and three colours: red, green and blue. Of course, these are just convenient terms, but perhaps knowledge is like that. Perhaps it is made up of different coloured and flavoured components which are present in different combinations in different kinds of knowledge.

There was no formal introduction on this first evening, and I was again aware of my lack of social skills. In my mind, I visualised these plastic people taking mingling courses, writing dissertations on and sitting exams in how to make pointless conversation and create the surface impression of competence. A useful skill, perhaps, but one that I nevertheless preferred not to possess. I yawned with my soft palate, keeping my mouth as closed as I could out of politeness. A large, painted lady with curly black hair and harpooned ears approached me, and I fought hard to resist an urge to weave my way to the opposite end of the room.

She elbowed her way through the chairs full of people, a homing missile with a mission. I tried not to meet her gaze, but her eyes were so ludicrous that I could not stop my own from feasting on them.

'Hello,' she said, directing herself at me and not Bryony in a way that made me wonder what I was doing to advertise myself as humiliation material.

'Hi,' I returned to her serve.

'I'm Helen.'

'Angel.'

'Pleased to meet you, Angel.'

I opened my mouth to reply, but she must have served an ace, and continued, 'Which branch are you from?'

'Branch? Oh, Newcastle. I've just...' I began, but she threw my racket out of the court.

'Nice to meet you.' She rushed off, bound for her next victim, rudely, without even a hint of a goodbye.

In a corridor up some flights of stairs was the room that I slept in for the first time that night; the room that would swallow up so much of my history in the weeks to come. As I flapped and bristled with the group of people in the lounge, or as they flapped and bristled around me, my bags sat alone and sunken in the vast bed, in much the same way that those I had left at home must have done. All of a sudden my life consisted of two piles of bags, hundreds of miles apart. Not only was I packed into bundles, but I was also separated into two distant clumps. No wonder I felt uneasy and disjointed.

The sheets were ivory-coloured and summer-thin, and brought shivers at night as the darkness rendered the sun ineffective. I was weary and hoped to fall asleep immediately, but my mind had other ideas. Social gatherings always bewildered me, and the evening's event had been no exception. It was difficult to bear the thought that these people would be my companions for the following weeks. They snorted at me through pretentious nostrils, squinted at me through their puss-ridden eyes. I knew that I did not belong with these people; and, not knowing whether this fact improved or deteriorated my position, I knew that I did not want to belong. They were monsters, hideous people, interested in self-preservation, self-motivation, self-glorification. I thought this was completely in contradiction with the aims of the course, but the others appeared not to spot any incongruity. As I dozed, I wondered if I was the only sane person left in the world.

The alarm clock called me to consciousness the following morning. I glanced at the curtains and saw only gloom on the other side of them, and my first thought was that my clock had broken and it was still night-time. I brushed my hair – grease-stricken with panic – out of my eyes, yawned soggily and went over to the window. It was light outside, but clouds of varying greys prevented the sun's long orange arms from reaching my window. The heavy rain contributed to this effect by making the air thick with dark globs of water. It was August and I had expected bright sunshine, too-hot days filled with the longing to get out of the indoors and into the outdoors. For a few moments I rested my elbows on the fakely marbled windowsill and gazed into the rain. If I stared hard enough I could make the plummeting drops disappear, but I could not make the sun break through the clouds. They were everywhere I looked, right into the far distance, crowning all that I saw.

I pulled my nightshirt more tightly around me, the weather outside making me feel chilly, even though the room was warmed by the artificial heat that flowed into it through the vents. Making myself a cup of coffee from the handy instant collection placed on a tray on the dressing table, I thought of Joe. He would probably still be asleep. I wished myself there with him, curled up in the swirling bedclothes. I should have been waking up for the first time in our new house, not in this sterile hotel room, alone, separated from him by an incomprehensibly vast space of places I did not know.

I dropped the powdered milk into the cup, shuddered slightly, and wrapped myself up cross-legged in the duvet. There were no pink flowers on the duvet at our new house. At home. The association between the little house in Durham and home seemed alien; I wanted to get back and live there. I felt trapped, lost, as if my life was disjointed and broken apart again. The tears wanted to come but I refused to let them this early in the day. It was essential that I got through this now. If I was going to give up, I should have done so long ago and saved myself and Joe this distress.

I showered the night out of my skin. The water dribbled from the plastic head on to my soft, dry shoulders, melting into bubbles as it hit the gel that I had smeared there. I closed my eyes and stood there feeling vulnerable as I always did when naked away from home, yet enjoying the soak and the sear of the hot water. The shower was confusing, as all showers tend to be, but it did not take me too long to work out that if I turned the handle towards the word 'HOT' that was printed in large red letters, the water would get colder. Conversely, turning towards the blue end of the dial would produce increasingly warmer water. The shower was a retreat; when I left I would have to go back into battle with Helen and the rest of the humiliation gang. As the air grew more and more humid, it began to enclose me in its sogginess, to whisper, 'Stay, stay,' seductively, until I almost rolled back to sleep.

Then I threw on some clothes. They were not the kind I was used to, and they hung awkwardly on my body. I wondered if anyone ever became accustomed to these restrictively shaped pieces of material. I wondered if anyone found they fitted into them neatly. They made me look fatter than I was, shorter than I was, and my head popped out of the collar of my shirt like that of a turtle from its shell. I wished I had tried harder to find something that would be acceptable and yet at the same time more in tune with me, but I remembered that finding the outfits I finally picked had been a hard enough task.

Particles make up everything in the universe, in the same way that numerous events make up a person's life. A particle has a property known as 'spin', which is denoted by a number. This number represents the number of times it has to be rotated before it looks the same; it is a kind of symmetry. Spin 0 means that it looks the same from any angle. Spin 1 particles must be spun all the way round once to look the same, and spin 2 particles only need to go for half a revolution; that is, in one revolution there are 2 positions in which a spin 2 particle looks the same from a given vantage point.

There are some particles which have a spin of ½. This is curious, as it means that they need to be rotated twice before they look the same. In other words, you can look at the same particle, the same object, from the same angle, but it will not look the same. Events in people's lives must have a spin of some infinitely small fraction, as they can be spun around eternally and never look the same as they did when you started. Today was the beginning of an event, or an infinitely divisible cluster of events, with a particularly tiny spin number. Moreover, it not only appeared symmetry-less in itself, but also seemed to throw this property on to all the other areas of my life, bestowing them with the same quality.

I was early; breakfast did not start for another quarter of an hour, so I sat on my bed, glowering at the evil stilettos in the corner of the room, and rested my head in my hands. I felt dizzy and bewildered and I wanted to talk to Joe. It was seven thirty in the morning, and it was unlikely that he would be awake. In any case, the phone in his – our – house had not yet been connected, so it was an impossible thought. Just for a moment I let myself imagine that he was there with me, that he would take me in his arms and magic luck and courage into me before I went into the battlefield. I could almost feel his firm hands on my shoulders, and again, I wanted to cry. Again, I held back the tears.

The breakfast room was gaudily decorated and enormous. Fake silver-coloured bowls and cutlery lay in waiting on the uninhibited, uninhabited tables. I looked around for a friendly place to sit. If I sat alone I would stand out, or worse, become swamped by enthusiastic chattering from 'new friends' come to join me. I scanned the room, and my eyes fell upon the woman who had sat next to me last night at the reception. At that moment, she looked up and invited me with a smile to join her. I psyched myself up and went over to her.

With the words, 'My name is Bryony,' she eroded the first barrier of friendship. I offered my own name before sitting down, and we shook hands.

'I didn't get to talk to you last night,' Bryony continued, and then confided, 'I suppose I was tired from the journey.'

I watched as she effortlessly lifted the grapefruit pieces out of the bowl and placed them one by one into her mouth, chewing slowly and automatically. I forced out a, 'Me too,' but my voice was clouded with the fuzz of my fraught nerves. We exchanged the questions that both had asked and answered over and over again the previous evening, but this time the same answers felt more meaningful.

How would I describe Bryony physically? I have captured every detail of her appearance in my mind, but I do not know how to put them all into words. She was in her late twenties – twenty-eight, I later discovered, just a few years older than me. I suppose she was petite in stature. Her personality made her appear strong and tall but without brashness. Her hair was long and brown and straight and slightly wispy, and hung down to just below her shoulders. Her mouth was large and welcoming, and her nose sat neatly beneath eyes that always seemed to glisten with her vital spirit.

It is unusual for people to be confident without arrogance, but Bryony managed it. I am deviating from a physical description, perhaps, but this quality was clear from the first glance. Her whole spirit was luminously and unselfconsciously displayed in her face for everyone to see. I don't think she did this deliberately – in fact, I don't know how that would have been possible – but she was so strong and alive that she could not avoid a physical manifestation of this incredible spirit.

People liked her. Few people are liked by everyone, but I saw no one take a dislike to Bryony. I felt honoured by the fact that she had chosen me to be her friend. She could have dived into the glittering yet boring conversation, become the centrepiece of any group she chose, yet she picked me as her friend. I feel a lump in my throat at this thought. Perhaps she felt sorry for me because I was alone while everyone else was crowing to each other; but that is an insult to her. She was genuine and she liked me, and I am very grateful for that.

Her neck was slender and usually hidden behind her hair, although she sometimes wore a neat ponytail. At such times one could see the soft, pale skin below her ears. At the bottom of her neck her skin curved out to become shoulders, collarbone, chest and back. The rest was covered, of course, by clothes – the secret shapes of her breasts, her torso and her legs – except her hands and sometimes her arms and ankles. Her hands showed by their lines and ridges that they had not been idle, and yet they had no roughness about them, no ugly coarseness. A few freckles were dotted over her arms, and she wore a small, black, plain wrist-watch.

During the last few days I spent with her, we had the most outrageous fun ever. Not outrageous in a bad or unusual sense but because they were fun. It seems to have been unusual for me to have had fun in my adult life. One Saturday we walked to the sea and threw pebbles into the whipped-up heads of water, the fine sand forcing its way into our shoes and between our toes. We laughed at the sandcastle we had built there in the first week. We laughed even more at the other, rival sandcastles.

Sand got in between our toes. Sand in our hair, soaring at us in the sea air, climbing our legs and attaching itself to our clothing. It must have been ticklish because we couldn't stop laughing. Sand clinging to our knees and elbows. We tried to brush it off each other's clothes there on the beach, but the more we got off, the more seemed to remain. Later, we tried to remove it back in our hotel rooms, but it seemed that nothing short of a shower was going to get rid of it. It gets under your skin, embeds itself in your pores, and you walk around with it like an itchy coating long after you have come away from the beach.

It was September, my favourite month of the year, and the warmest day since we had been in Cornwall. We walked right up to where the little waves were breaking, and Bryony threatened to push me in.

'And that's supposed to scare me?' I flashed at her. The water was less than a shoe sole deep, and grasped around our feet, trying to wet us, trying to mingle with the sand, to form a seaside cocktail, but too small to succeed. She narrowed her eyes playfully, and we walked on. I stared at my feet, looking at the pink shells that littered the beach, feeling warm and happy.

'Are you thinking about Joe again?' she asked, mock seriously, waiting for me to say something that would open me to her affectionate ridicule.

'No,' I confessed, almost reluctantly. 'Just feeling... well, happy.'

She touched her hand lightly on my shoulder. 'Good!'

I smiled at her; I had started to feel that I loved her.

At Nottingham I had taken my studies more seriously than anything, even perhaps than my relationship with Joe. Sheffield and Manchester had seen me as a serious young student, shoulders weighed down with intriguing books, and no time to see the world. In Peterborough I was merely miserable. But now, as I got to know Bryony, I almost felt that I was free. There was no exam to pass, no standards to meet, for once. The only thing I had to do was last the eight weeks, and it would be over. I told myself early on that I would only get through it if I allowed myself, even forced myself, to have fun as well. Bryony made this easy.

We weren't wild. We didn't spend all night out at clubs drinking and bopping and flirting with men, or go out on extravagant spending sprees. We didn't do any of the things that most people would consider to be outrageous, and yet there was something distinctly decadent about the way we spent our time together, increasingly so as it winged past. Bryony made me happy, despite myself, despite the fact that I was so far away from Joe, despite the fact that I had been anticipating only misery in Penzance.

It frightened me that the others took the course so seriously. Bryony's sympathies were with me. We laughed and joked about the people giving the course and about our fellow 'prisoners'. We made all kinds of stupid observations, and in the evenings we would roll about the floor with laughter in her room or mine as we played at being these people.

'What about the way that really fat man tried to play the tambourine?' she giggled on one occasion. She got up from the bed and, taking a bottle of hairspray from the dressing table, started waving it around and jiggling her hips in imitation.

'Oh, wait! I'll be his crony,' I said, picking up a spoon and singing into the reflective microphone. 'Don't go awa-a-ay,' I crooned badly.

'Find it in your heart to sta-a-ay,' she joined in, both of us now hardly able to sing for our tittering. She came up to me and put her arm around me so that we could wander around the room joined at the hip, singing in mock drunkenness, and banging percussively on the surfaces as we passed them. I suppose we were cruel but neither of us had come across anything so artificial and ridiculous before. We were simply venting our incredulity.

Often we sat up until well into the early hours talking, some-times jokingly, sometimes in earnest. She told me about her passion for Egypt.

'You must have seen pictures of the pyramids?'

'Yes, of course.'

'Well,' she grinned, 'they are nothing like that. They are so huge and so unique that there is no way you can capture them on film.'

'Oh. So I should throw away all those pictures I have of them all over my walls?'

'Yes,' she mocked. 'Really, they are enormous. When you stand next to them you can see the individual bricks, and they are so large you can't imagine how the Ancient Egyptians could have dragged a single one across the sand, never mind built them into a huge pyramid.'

'I'd love to go there.'

'Oh, you really should,' she enthused, suddenly deeply seri-ous. 'There's such a feeling of... I don't know what. An incredible air of history, of the newness of civilisation, a sense of a completely different world.' She fell silent, and I could see that she was thinking of the golden deserts, the temples and the tombs of that distant civilisation. 'I will go there again as soon as I can,' she said suddenly, 'and you must come too.'

I smiled. 'I think I need to do a bit of saving first... but yes, I'd love to. Especially now that you've done such a good job of selling the place to me. What are you, a travel agent?'

For some reason she took my hand and pressed it between hers. I don't know why but it was the right thing to do at that moment. Maybe it was because she was opening her heart to me and I hadn't thought her crazy or obsessive, and she wanted to show her appreciation. Perhaps it was just a further stage in the bond that was rapidly developing between us.

I am rushing ahead; the early days were not like that. In the dark ages of our knowing each other we were still nervous and rather taut in our conversations. It all looks very petty now, glancing over my shoulder at those first days. The talk of our lives, of Joe, of everything that was close and important to us, that seemed so serious then, becomes demoted into an inky cloud of insignificance in comparison to subsequent events. I hardly believe now that neither of us expected any of it. Now, as I retrace the steps we took towards the dreadful climax, those quick, downhill strides, I look for the point where it was too late to turn back, or for a catalyst, for anything that might explain events to me – as if the catastrophe was somehow of our own making – but, of course, I find none.

I remember the glint in her eye when I first mentioned Joe to her; the 'tell-me-more' inflexion in the tilt of her head. I had never had to talk to anyone about Joe before, and it was interesting to me that I found it difficult. My friends at Nottingham had seen the relationship develop from the start and knew everything there was to know about Angel-and-Joe. Starting the story from the beginning, however, was a different matter, despite the fact that there was nothing remotely complicated to consider. I remember feeling relieved that it was Joe I had to describe to her, and not Alan or Justin.

Joe had focused me, for perhaps the first time in my life. Nottingham was an exciting and curious way to spend three years, but I had begun with no idea where I would be afterwards. Now I knew that I wanted to stay with Joe, that he would be the centre of my life. I met him just after Easter in his final year, my second. He told me afterwards that he thought I looked young and pretty and had sought for some time to be my friend because of these qualities. He looked awkward when I told him my age, which made me laugh inwardly; he was surprised to find that I was older than him. But still he pursued me.

Bryony tilted her head at this point in my story, murmuring something about the sweetness of new love, an almost mocking smile on her face.

'Yes, it was sweet,' I admitted, and she propped her face up in her hands. 'But after a couple of months he finished and went to a job in Durham, and I was left in Nottingham without him.' I sighed, and then added, 'Without him – where I have been ever since.'

She said nothing, and I told her of my efforts to find a job near him, my determination to locate myself firmly and permanently next to him, and my frustration at having to spend the first months of our lives together so definitively far apart.

'But it is only a few weeks!' she encouraged. 'And then it will all be over and you will have him for the rest of your life!' She made light of my dilemma, not in a cruel and unsympathetic way, but as a means of support. It struck me that she was right.

I smiled. 'Yes, I am lucky, I suppose,' I said, and my expression must have given away my thoughts all too vividly. She asked me to describe him.

'How do I describe him? He's tall and he has soft, curly hair, and he's mine!' I ventured. She laughed.

What more was there to say? His eyes are sea green, his hair is a light brown with subtle red lights when the sun catches it, and he is almost six feet tall. But these are details, random facts strewn on a page. I love Joe, and this makes him unique and incomprehensible to anyone but me.

When we were first together, we were rather frightened of each other. I suppose I was reluctant to fall in love with him. I still felt far too close to the Alan/Justin crisis and to Peterborough to expose myself to such risks again; it had been two years, but the experience had left me fragile and somewhat crippled emotionally. But in the end I found it impossible to stay distant. We lived just a short bound from each other, and in those first weeks we spent most of our time in each other's rooms, or sometimes just walking aimlessly around the campus. The first time we went into town together I was terrified. I have always found shopping to be something that is best enjoyed alone, but we were so absorbed in each other that we hardly noticed the shops, the streets or the roads at all. We passed window displays of jeans, chocolate and CDs, the inviting open doors of department stores, the enticing, wafting scents of toffee and fudge, and for once none of this managed to penetrate me. We just walked around, scorning the shops, pigeons at our feet, floating effortlessly up the hills, without really knowing where we went.

He put back into me what Manchester, Peterborough, Justin

and Alan had sucked from me. Not only was I in love with him but some of this love began to reflect off his mirror surface, back on to me. He showed me that I was not worthless, that I was not incompetent and incapable, and also that I could let myself feel things like a real person again. I became aware that I had been avoiding depression by simply disallowing all emotions for some time, and I actually began to crave mental sensation. He proved to me that I was capable of love, of intimacy and closeness, of all the things that I had blamed my lack of for my previous disasters.

When I told him about my past and why I had left Manchester, I thought he would be disgusted with me, but he just held me in his arms and pressed his face close to mine, wordlessly, and I felt his sympathy, his understanding, exuding from his pores. I told him about my illness in Peterborough – my Samaritans training had taught me to think of it as an illness rather than a defect – and he showered me with sympathy that was wholesome and not patronising. I felt full of Joe, a cat full of the finest cream, and I had to lick my whiskers occasionally to remind myself that the sumptuous sensation was real.

Bryony was unattached, and enjoying it. She told me about her flat by the River Wey, and her life seemed idyllic to me. She made being single seem like something I had always wanted, and I began to wonder if maybe, secretly, it was. I had never felt any real uneasiness about my relationship with Joe before now, which was odd considering the dramatic failures I had experienced in my previous encounters, but suddenly I realised that I was feeling some kind of doubt. There was something in the way this girl spoke, the free and easy way her hair wisped behind her as she walked – no ties, nothing to fear. It wasn't anything she said; only that she put into my head the fear that I was about to become a trapped woman, willingly leading myself into a prison cell. A cell, where togetherness would degenerate and deteriorate into something rank and grotesque, where chains would appear around my ankles and wrists, my personality shaved from me like hair from my head.

I remembered what being alone was truly like, when the envious friends had gone out with or home to their husbands and lovers and all there was left to do was sit alone in the house and turn the television up loud to drown out the silence. It was the silence that had really got to me. I could manage being by myself, and in fact I was glad of it some of the time, but when everything went quiet I would start to feel nervous. After I left Justin I lived alone for several months. I would go home after my day at the market stall and quake at the thought of another night single and defenceless, another sleep racked by dreams of intruders and extreme sensitivity to every sound. Even during the day I wanted noise. I wanted bustle and to have other people in my world, even if I did not actually interact with them, which usually I did not. This is partly why I went out every day and why I became a Samaritan.

But Bryony made singleness so much more attractive. Perhaps it suited her more than it suited me. I don't know, but she almost made me want it. Either that, or I had been secretly – secretly in the sense that I did not know about it myself – having fears about the commitment I was making to Joe for some time. I am still not sure which way round it happened, but a few ragged doubts began to form among the olive trees and sunshine of our coupledom. I dismissed them, of course, very successfully by day, but in the dark of night when I was cold and alone, I had to admit that they were there.

I suppose I let Bryony see more of myself than I had meant to, simply because it was unavoidable. I felt her to be an ally: it was me and her against the rest of the world, against the petty sessions we had to attend each day and the brain-numbing roles we were required to force ourselves into in the name of character-building. I tried to tell myself that there was some point to this, that I would one day find something I gained from it useful, but it was impossible. I knew that I was learning nothing. I missed Joe, as much as I ever had, and I felt deeply the irony of being apart from him for the longest time ever just as we had begun to live together. Bryony listened patiently to my wailing and comforted me, and I could not help but share my tears as well as my thoughts with her. I felt alone and tearful without Joe. I was already letting Bryony into my heart; she was there and Joe was not.

After breakfast on the first day there was bowling. It felt

ludicrous to be playing games with a group of people in business-like suits and of varying ages and dispositions. Most of them managed to hide the fact that they felt like fools, but I was unable to do this. I suppose that is what it was about – an ice-breaking activity – yet I could not throw myself into it. I had already decided that the whole thing was going to be a waste of time and again I was loath to prove myself wrong.

I watched the easy way that Bryony sent the balls sliding down the alley. She had obviously done this before, and I was transfixed by the way that her arm elegantly swooped the ball to the starting position, the way she released it almost imperceptibly, the moment when it left her hand difficult to spot. Her arm continued in a large arc and hardly came to rest by her side before the ball had reached the other end of the lane and deftly demolished all or most of the pins. There were a few other champion bowlers there but when their pins fell down they rattled garrulously, falling randomly and violently in a mess. Bryony's lay down for her by an effort of will, as though they bowed to her, as gently and elegantly as her own deft movements, yet as definitively as those of the large men who must have had tattoos hidden beneath their padded suit shoulders.

'I suppose you think this is going to be easy, then?' I threw at her, trying to remain polite whilst demonstrating to her that I was capable of humour. I thought it hadn't worked very well, but she seemed perceptive enough to understand my intention.

'Oh, it's just luck! Sometimes I do okay, other times I do really badly.'

'But you won! I'm impressed.'

She smiled. 'There will be other things that you'll win at. And if you like, I'll teach you how to bowl, if there's time.'

She was serious, but I ventured, 'Are you implying that I'm useless at this?'

'Yes.' She had beaten me with my own stick, or rather tickled me with my own feather, since there was no hostility involved, and I smiled simply at her.

There must have been a surplus of coffee in Cornwall because it was forced down us at every conceivable opportunity. I had never seen so many kinds, either. I think this was supposed to impress upon us the wealth and grandeur of the company we were about to work for. Perhaps it was an attempt to fill us full-to-bursting with caffeine so that we would not fall asleep during all the boring talks and slide-shows, but that certainly did not work for me. I might have been awake but concentration eluded me.

Bryony and I walked into the huge function room and sat down together, as the president of the company walked up to the pathetic little platform at the front of the room. He adjusted his ludicrous bow tie and opened his mouth as if to speak in a grand, booming voice that would make us all sit up straight and absorb ourselves in his every word.

'Hello, everyone,' he squeaked. 'I hope those of you who arrived yesterday had a good night's sleep, and the rest of you had good journeys.' Then, with hardly a pause for breath, he launched himself into his pre-prepared spiel. 'I know that you are all very different people and will be doing very different jobs, but I want you all to hold on to the fact that from this time forth you have one very important thing in common – you all work for me.'

I think he wanted us to laugh, and a few people at the back of the room tittered obligingly, but nobody found him funny.

He continued. 'The activities in which you will be taking part have all been designed by experienced team-building experts, and, as you will probably have guessed, this is the main purpose of your sojourn here. We want you to feel like an important brick in the company wall, an indispensable component, a link in the chain of the machine.'

The room was enormous, and nowhere near filled by its occupants. Moreover, the president was not a large man, and he could not have picked a worse venue in which to make himself look imposing. By even this early stage, no one had the slightest bit of respect for him. Bryony and I turned to scrutinise each other's faces simultaneously and we both saw a mock seriousness turn immediately to a suppressed giggle.

Next, we were led into a room that contained a large number of chairs arranged around the walls of the room, giving the impression of a day room in a residential home, the only difference being that the chairs were identical to one another.

Some people moved towards the chairs, but Mr President screeched, 'No, don't sit on the chairs, please.' I am sure he grinned secretly to himself as the embarrassed culprits darted as far away from any chairs as they could get without, as they thought, incriminating themselves.

'I want you to sit in a circle around the books,' he directed, indicating a huge, messy pile of books in the middle of the floor. There were quite a few looks of dismay at having to sit on the floor. A lot of the people there thought that they were too important, too superior or too old, even though none of them could have been older than forty. Bryony and I crossed our legs on the floor, and, as I sat down, I wondered what the point of this was going to be. I thought that we might to be asked to burn them in some bizarre display of company loyalty, but thankfully I was wrong.

'Have a good rummage through; see what we have found for you. Then, I want you to pick one each. Something that interests you.' There was a pause in which nobody moved, and I smiled enquiringly at Bryony, then a tall fat man reached into the pile and started looking at the titles. Satisfied that they were not the first, everyone else now joined in, and the room was silent but for the sound of books being pulled out from underneath each other and replaced, pages turning, spines cracking, crackling, cackling.

I thought this session might give me a clue about Bryony, about what interested her, what she liked. I wondered if this was the point of the exercise – to get to know our colleagues in a slightly more subtle way than the potted life-history sessions I had heard about – but I wanted to be the only one to glean such facts about her. I looked on out of the corner of my eye as she systematically sorted through the books, picking up one and turning a few pages from time to time. Some of them looked very old, some even began to fall apart as we handled them, and others were new and cheap. There were tourist guides, cookery manuals, academic textbooks, literature new and old, picture books; the variety was immense.

★

The kittenless girl stands crying in the street. The tall grown-ups flit past, paying no attention to her weeping. Children are always crying, they think. One of her red shoes is caked in mud, and her hair has been tangled by the tears that she has brushed into the long strands. She sits down on the pavement, still searching with her eyes for her malicious brothers. They must be far away by now, or they could be back in their garden, playing with the cat, teasing it, frightening it. She does not know. She could look for them again, but she knows that they will always win. She knows that beating her again and again will only delight them, so she does not move. She is wise for her years and thoughtful. She visualises her cat in many dreadful plights. She wonders what she should do. She cannot go home, as her brothers will taunt her, will plague her, will be cruel to the cat to make her cry. So she gets up on to her feet and starts walking through the streets, away from her house.

★

I envied Bryony the way the words flowed off her tongue. I had been bored almost silly listening to the others reading out their selected passages from the books we had chosen before lunch, but hearing Bryony read was a pleasure. My book was a rather old copy of *Gray's Anatomy*. The body had always fascinated me, and I fingered the soft, dark cover lightly, occasionally checking that my place mark had not fallen out – it would be my turn to read soon. My eyes fell on to the mass of veins, arteries and glands underneath my fingers, and I let them rest there as I listened to Bryony.

'Egypt was not the first civilisation, but it is one that has caught and captivated the mass attention of the modern public in a way that completely outstrips its less famous predecessor, Mesopotamia.' The curt style did not really suit her lips, yet she rolled out the words as naturally as if they had been her own. 'The pyramids, the sole survivor from the Seven Wonders of the World, are a miraculous testimony to their skill, both in terms of design and creation, and also in those of sheer mobilisation of labour.'

If I stared into her mouth I could see her tongue making the syllables against her teeth and her palate. I watched for some time, trying to ascertain what it was about these actions that made her speech so musical and so easy, but I did not succeed. I hardly noticed when she finished speaking. Then she was moving towards me, back to her seat, and I pulled myself up sharply and pushed my hair behind my ears; it was my turn next. I clambered over the laps of some dumpy-looking people, swallowed hard as I stood in front of them, and began to stumble over my words.

'The Shoulder is an enarthrodial or ball-and-socket joint,' I began in my best medical tone. 'The bones entering into its formation are the large globular head of the humerus, received into the shallow glenoid cavity of the scapula, an arrangement which permits of very considerable movement, whilst the joint itself is protected against displacement by the strong ligaments and tendons which surround it, and above by an arched vault, formed by the under surface of the coracoid and acromion processes, and the coracto-acromial ligament.' I thought of Joe's shoulders as I read. I thought about how the skin around them is soft and spongy and then draws itself gradually to the rounded apex of the shoulder bone, where it is pulled taut and smooth. I like to kiss his shoulders, and I like him to kiss mine. They are an underrated part of the body. Shoulders are erotic.

Sometimes when we make love I find my eyes looking over his shoulder while my mouth kisses the skin there. My lips brush gently over the tight skin and touch him only lightly, soundlessly. From such a vantage I can see the heels of his feet pointing at the ceiling, and also his buttocks clenching and grinding as he pushes himself into me. It is an almost circular motion, and I like to watch it through the veil of my exertion, the haze of sex that puts a film over the eyes and a cover around the ears, shutting out everything but the lovemaking.

I checked myself, my expression, my stance, hoping that my face had not given my thoughts away, and a quick glance around the room convinced me that I was safe. I reached the end of the passage gratefully, and rejoined my seat.

'Historian?' I enquired over dinner that evening, glancing at the book that lay on the table next to Bryony's elbow. We had been given the books we had chosen to read from that afternoon – another benevolent gift to demonstrate to us the munificence of the organisation we had been so fortunate to join. *Gray's Anatomy* was safely put to bed in a drawer in my room.

'Yes, how did you guess?' she smiled back at me.

'I was impressed earlier, you know. Is there anything you can't do?'

She looked slightly blank, and I continued, 'Your reading...?' It occurred to me that I might have been the only person whom her words – or rather the borrowed words that she poured from her lips – had so affected, and I began to feel very embarrassed.

'Oh... thank you. I've never felt I was very good at it.'

'You are! All of a sudden I want to know everything about Egypt.'

'It is a fascinating subject. Have you been there?'

'What? In my state of poverty?'

Now it was her turn to experience embarrassment – I could tell that Egypt was so important to her that she couldn't imagine not having been there. 'You must, as soon as you can,' she enthused. 'It's the most fascinating place.' I imagined going there with Bryony. I pictured her in the khaki shorts and white shirt of the archaeologist, leading me around the ancient monuments. The desert, the sand. We would need no guide, and she would take me away from the tourist traps to her favourite, quiet places (for somehow I knew that her favourite places would be quiet ones), briefing me on their fascinating history. Bryony the historian.

I stabbed a potato with my sparkling fork, and Bryony put the equivalent question to me. 'And you studied... biology?' she guessed, turning her gaze into a smiling squint as if she could see into my brain.

'No,' I replied. 'Well, yes, for a term and a half, a long time ago...' I trailed off, then added, 'And then I did German for slightly longer, and finally settled down to counselling, which I actually finished.'

'Wow! You have a lot of talents!'

'No, that's just the problem. It took me a while to find something I could actually do.'

'You are just too modest,' she flashed at me, and all I could do was smile. 'So,' she continued, 'what does a counsellor do in a company like this?'

'Oh, you know they have company counsellors?' She evidently didn't, so I continued. 'A lot of companies of this size do nowadays, you know.' I was plugging my own career, so I silenced myself, and Bryony did not speak either. It was a moment that could easily have been tremendously awkward, but for some reason it was not. The clattering and ugliness of mass eating continued around us and we sat in stillness and silence, easily, comfortably, finding nothing to say but finding also no need to speak.

★

The little girl continues to shift her feet heavily through the streets. She is not sure where she has got to, but still she continues walking, turning random corners, doubling back on herself without knowing she is doing so, all the time the tears shooting out of their ducts. At first she passes many familiar places: the sweet shop, the post office, the field where some of her friends run with their dogs in the evenings; but then the territory becomes wholly unfamiliar. Her walk turns into quite a journey, but she mostly doesn't notice her surroundings.

She does not know how far she walks but she knows that they will be cross at home if they find that she has been out alone for this long, so with her child's straightforward sense of direction and homing spirit, she turns her steps back in on themselves and soon finds herself back in her garden. She is still crying, and there is no sign of Marcus and Daniel.

★

History is always in the past. People sometimes wonder why we bother with it, since it is already dead and buried, yet it has an enormous bearing on the present and the future. History is a precondition for everything we know. A person consists not only of their memories but also their history: their parents, their childhood, their experiences. Their parents are governed by their own histories too, which means that every living person is the consequence of a chain of histories and not just of their own personal history. All of existence is a line stretching all the way back to the primordial event, whatever that might be, and we are thus all descended from a single microsecond, a fraction of a microsecond. Perhaps this begins to explain why two people sometimes feel a great affinity with one another the way I started to feel inexorably drawn to Bryony that evening.

Night

Beethoven. The composer who could not hear. The bad-tempered jester who, one hundred and fifty years on, still fills our ears with the mellowest, the gentlest, the most volatile. He described himself as a *Tondichter*, and was indeed a poet of tones, the leader of a great, shining, magical dance, shaping sound into the fantastic, the grotesque, the utterly nimble.

There must be a *Geschichtedichter*, a *Zeitdichter*, some kind of dancer who can take the fluidity of time and history and twist it into whatever shapes are required. I once thought, fantastically, that it was me. I used to think that my history didn't work in the way that other people's did, that I made my own decisions and broke out of the flow of events into my own little dances. I thought I made choices about my life, that I was different from all the others who are blindly pushed and twizzled whichever way the winds might decide.

It feels like dusk. The train has been swallowed up by Paddington Station; or the daylight by some larger animal, and there is none left to see by. I rub my eyes and look out of the window again, but all I see is my own reflection. I rub my eyes once more, as I realise I look tired and worn out. I am glad I am wearing no make-up, as it would have run by now into a swirl of colours down my cheeks. It might be nice to have a rainbow-coloured face; I would look like a clown and I might be able to cheer people up. The people at Paddington look as though they have not smiled for a long time. The frowns are cemented into their cheekbones, their facial muscles taut and inflexible, taught to be inflexible. The loneliness of the long-distance runner is here transmuted into a different kind of loneliness, a different kind of running.

People everywhere but not a drop of friendly human spirit to drink. Not a friendly face in sight, only enemies to battle with, to shove aside, elbows everywhere, hard, strong commuting shoes crushing your toes if you are not endlessly vigilant. And they are running, not for enjoyment or even in order to achieve anything, but because it is the only life they know. Would the rats that live in the tunnels beneath London, battered day and night by the rush of the trains, live there if they knew about the sunshine and greenery they could feast on outside? Here they know only scavenging and foraging and running about in the dark, getting away from trains. But they do not miss green fields and fresh, live insects, as they have never known this life. I am sure the commuters on the tube are similarly blinkered. They have heard of other lives but somehow they think that theirs is better. It is a kind of vanity, I suppose.

I felt that Bryony was my friend already. I went to my room thinking of her on that second night, but when I got into bed it was Joe who was on my mind. I wondered what he would be doing. Ten o'clock – it was quite early for bed. My day had been exhausting, and I knew I would sleep well, but Joe would probably be fully awake and working on some project. I imagined him sitting in the large shed at the bottom of the garden; at last, somewhere he could take his tools and his wood and work without having to clear up after himself. He would have made it inhabitable by now, I was sure, even though the house would be far from satisfactory. He might even be working in the kitchen, which made me shudder, but I told myself that I would not mind as long as he tidied up for my return, which I knew he would do.

I like to watch Joe with his planks and lumps of wood and his sharp carving tools. It is miraculous the way he can take a shapeless, featureless block and coax it into something beautiful. I have seen other wood sculptures but none of them are as full of life, as real, as Joe's. Sometimes he carves ladies, girls, with swishing skirts and flowing hair. It is as though he has captured them in the middle of a movement; there is nothing static about the figures, nothing wooden. I expect them to continue turning, walking, running, to burst into full human life.

Sometimes he makes functional things. He has quite a skill with cupboards and chairs as well as with slices of life captured in wood. I have run my fingers across the veneers of his cupboards in the past, I have opened and closed the doors and been impressed with the way that they slide effortlessly in and out of their catches. The shelves are fitted into the unit seamlessly and the hinges are hardly visible. He has sold chairs and cupboards, and his work is very attractive, but his sculpture is where his real essence lies.

His figures seem to have a personality. Even though their heads are usually faceless, they nevertheless appear to have expressions. It is in the seeming fluidity of their bodies, their hair and their movement, even though they are formed out of lifeless wood. Like Beethoven, he is something of a Prometheus, and although his creations are caught in a single moment of their lives, I think those lives are no less real. They have pasts and futures just like the rest of us; it is just that their present over-whelms them, in much the same way that all our presents do.

This is what Joe did with me. I realised the analogy long ago. I was a lifeless block of wood when we met. I had some shape, a little more than his usual starting material, I have to admit, but I was nothing compared to what he has made me. I sometimes think of myself with an almost narcissistic pride, but it is Joe's skill that I am marvelling at, not anything of my own doing. His hands are magical, life-breathing creatures, that can traverse any shell and make it alive.

I try to move slowly but London makes this impossible. There is always an earlier tube train, always some irascible reason for getting to your destination that little bit sooner. So I try to move quickly but find that I am held up by the masses of people who are trying to do the same.

Night is a time for sleeping. It is also a time for worrying, for regret, for catching up with all the difficulties that we throw into our future during the daylight hours. And thirdly, the night is full of stars, like it was on that night I walked along the river with Bryony. The little silver dots seemed to draw the sky down on to us so that it enveloped us totally in its nightness. We felt as though there was no civilisation and no world other than the dark sky and the shiny points. Night indoors is very different from the same hours out of doors. Inside you can switch on the lights, or even light candles, close the curtains, put the heating on and curl up, safe from the darkness and the elements outside the doors and windows. Outside you can smell the air and hear the nocturnal sky. The world is different in darkness. Human lighting contraptions go none of the way towards turning night into day. It is a different place, where we say and do different things and feel different emotions.

'*Paddington will be the first railway station to receive a major overhaul that will propel it into the ranks of one of the world's first-class stations,*' screams the brochure in my hands. I look around and above me at the enormous shell and read on. It is a Grade I listed building and yet they are planning to deface it by the addition of a mezzanine which they will fill with shops and separate from the trains by means of a huge chunk of glass. It looks like it is also going to become something of a conference centre. I suppose it is already full enough of business people to justify this, but the idea is a startling one.

I trawl through the heavy text, absorbing its details: platform widening; skyscraper-style office buildings; better access to tubes. Newcastle, too, is currently being renovated – the walls and the huge roof. The stopping points of destinations are being revitalised. The points of recognition in my life are being altered beyond recognition, and if I think about it this makes me feel very unstable. Many of the defining points of a human life are physical landmarks, as well as the emotional and chronological flashpoints that comprise all of us.

Slowly, yawning, I peeled off my plain black suit and the new burgundy shirt – another one that I had bought especially for the occasion. Are the majority of people who stay in hotels vain creatures, or are the endless mirrors simply an attempt to make the rooms look larger? In any case, I could not help fixing my eyes on the image of myself in my underwear. Old, tatty underwear – I had not thought it worth buying anything new, since no one but me would see the garments that clung to me beneath my outer layer of acceptable drapes. It was my trusty old bra, the dark green one with little embroidered flowers filling every spare millimetre of material. It looked as though the flowers were multiplying, had run out of space, and would spill out, creeping on to my body, tattooing my flesh. I smiled to myself, thinking of the number of times I had removed this bra for Joe. I closed my eyes as I took it off once again, alone this time, and tried to recapture from my mind the feel of Joe's hot, wanting eyes burning into me, taking me in, as if I was new to him, as he did even now.

It is wonderful to feel so needed. I am not sure whether or not Justin ever felt like that about me, but if he did he was completely incapable of expressing it. Alan was passionate; my heart still skipped at the thought of Alan, but it was only ever dark and bad. We never had the chance to try a 'real' relationship. We were always jumping into doorways, hiding in the dark, concealing the love and passion we felt for one another. It might have burnt out in a very short time had I chosen to stay with him, or it might have disappeared the moment it became legitimate. I suppose that was one of the fears that prompted me to run away. Either way, it had never been as it was now with Joe.

I looked over at my nightshirt hanging on the wall. The air in my room was cold, but I felt the need to press the sheets against my naked body, to have them stroke and bathe my skin. I climbed into bed, tucked myself up in the abundant folds of the sheets and sighed. I wished Joe had a telephone. I wanted to hear his voice, the deep, soothing tones comfortingly at the other end of the springy coils that led from the telephone by my bed to the little hole in the wall, into which they vanished.

I love the way the sound of his voice makes my body feel. Every pore, every atom of my skin springs to life when he speaks. I become suddenly aware of my clothes, that they are not part of me. Aware that they hide skin which never sees the sunlight, curves and lines that thrill to his touch. His voice slides down from my ear, over my neck, my shoulders. It clings to my body, covering it, encasing it, possessing it. My breathing changes. Colours around me become brighter, edges soften. His vocal chords are fingers that touch and tease my body. The sound of his breath, a zephyr driving away all that separates me from him. The air leaving his lips blows away the stagnant facts of reality, makes me feel, makes me want.

If the engineers from the telephone company came to connect him now, that hole would be the way to Joe, I thought. I could talk to him, I could watch my voice disappearing into the wall, and maybe, if I made a concerted effort, I could follow the words as they flew to his ear. It would not be very far by that route; my voice would reach him almost instantly – a time machine. I pictured myself being pulled into the plastery hole, pulled towards Joe by some enormous magnetic power, emerging at the receiver in his hand, startling him, kissing him before he could realise what had happened.

The phone bill would be enormous, as I would have to make the return journey when he put the phone down, and this I would be reluctant to do. The *swoosh* back into the wire, the black hole draw of the telephone in my hotel room. I wondered what would happen if someone walked into my room and, seeing no one there, cut the connection. Would I be lost in telespace for ever? Would I roam the cables and the airwaves like a ghost – a ghost of technology? I would haunt conversations from now until the end of the world. A crossed line, only I would be real, inside the telephone.

★

A tap on the shoulder awakes her from her babyish reverie. She has been thinking of how the stones that are sunk into the path have fallen in different places. She is thinking how strange this is when she watched her own father drop large clumps of them at a time from the same source. She has been trying to imagine them falling from the sky into the unset concrete, jostling with each other, some taking a vertical path downwards, others travelling in the shape of a rainbow, thrown further so that they landed in a different spot. She decides that her father must be very clever to sow the stones in this way. She feels the tap on her shoulder and turns abruptly to find Marcus and Daniel standing tall above her. They shift to stand by her side. Their combined shadow soaks up any parts of the sun's light that try to reach her. Trapped by their darkness, she tries to read the message in their faces, but can only tell that they are here to hurt her again. 'Where do you think we have hidden your cat?' asks Daniel. His slight lisp robs his words of the dramatic effect he is trying to achieve. The girl neither moves nor answers, but her brothers continue. 'We are not going to hurt it any more. All you have to do is find it.' 'We will help you,' Marcus adds blithely. 'It will be fun, like hide and seek.' Their sister considers for a moment. She does not want to join in with their spiteful games and she is frightened of the names they call her simply because they are older than her, but she wants to find her cat.

★

It is dark on the tube train. They try to make it light by putting little fluorescent tubes-of-daylight all along the curved ceilings. They try to make us think of other things by pasting bad poems and holiday adverts on the walls, but it does not work. It is so dark outside that the windows behave like mirrors and we can see ourselves in them. I look distorted; there is almost two of me, but the images are not quite coherent enough, and instead my lines and features appear fuzzy and crazy to me. A mass of lines, a mess of lines etched in the darkness on the other side of the glass.

Bryony left my head in a fuzzy, crazy mess. I miss her. There is so much I wanted to do with her, so much of my life I wanted to share with her. There is no point in this desperation. Nothing can be achieved now that the damage is done, but still my guilt remains. And Joe. I am almost home and in his arms, but I am light years from seeing Bryony again; will I ever? Is it all right to miss her more than I do Joe at this juncture? This is a complete feeling of withoutness, permanent, unresolvable. My journey both away from and towards Joe is almost at an end. It is almost the time for me to cease to miss him, but when will I be able to say that about Bryony?

Imagine a train journey between stations that can move at any time. Imagine a rail network built around stations that are not stationary. Un-stations, moving goalposts. Timetables would be useless. Destinations would be random. You could look out of the window and see your station in the distance, if you were lucky. The train draws ever nearer, you collect together your belongings. You get to your feet and move towards the doors. Then the station is gone. The platform dissolved. The tracks endless. It would be an enormous trick of chance to reach any station at all, and to reach the destination you wanted would be almost impossible.

I never quite got to Bryony. I never quite reached her. I began a journey towards her but I did not make the destination in time, and there will be no compensation for the delay, no money back. The curious thing is that I still don't know what that destination would have been, or whether it would itself have been merely a passing place on the way to something more permanent. I think I would have liked to find out. Perhaps I can continue my travels without her. I don't know if I can manage it, or even if I want to, but I do know that she has given me a starting push down a new road that I have not seen before and that there are exciting and exotic places at the end of it. The only thing stopping me, I think, is that she won't be there.

Training

I shivered. The yellow sun was casting its beams through the polished windows, but they landed on the other side of the room, merely making me feel chilly in contrast to the bright patch on the facing wall. The room was filled with the same fresh-faced recruits who seemed to have lost none of their fake vitality, and I wondered how they managed to muster up such enthusiasm. I certainly felt none myself. The fat man at the front of the room was introducing himself. He wore a white suit and his eyes were huge and bloating, American-style, like almost everything I had encountered here so far. I was dismayed at this; I had always thought of Cornwall as a quiet, Celtic place, full of piskies and pasties. I wanted to find beaches and caves and vast stretches of violent sea, not to be trapped in a stagy room following someone's dreamt-up business plan.

The activities never ceased. The booklet had warned that it would be intensive, and this was certainly true. Even our so-called leisure hours were planned and agendicised. We ate breakfast together in a large room every day, and sometimes there were screens piping out endless company information, or large men in odd suits who stood at the front of the room and competed to be heard with the crunching of the cereals. I have never been a particularly noisy eater, but at such times I discovered the pleasure of grinding the flakes into my teeth as slowly and violently as I could, crashing my incisors down on them so that they made a sound like a distant explosion.

Sometimes I thought of Joe eating breakfast alone in our house. Perhaps he would eat at work, or maybe not at all, but I liked to visualise him at the big round table in the kitchen crunching the marmalade on to his toast with a big flat knife and placing it between his teeth, chewing, chewing, and finally sending it down into the winding tubes of his digestive system. Every now and then I felt a faint stab of panic that he might be sitting at our table with somebody else, another girl that he had found himself to alleviate the pain of being away from me. I trusted Joe infinitely but I could not stop my mind from playing such tricks on me. And after all, I knew that he equally trusted me, and I was beginning to wonder if I was worthy of that trust.

I was missing him intensely. I found every moment of those first few weeks almost unbearable because I was so far from him. Yet at the same time there were new doubts. They crept up on me wormily, sliding around in my stomach and gradually getting their way right into each of my veins so that I could no longer ignore them. Sometimes when I thought of him I felt that dull ache in my stomach that told me I was doing the wrong thing. Yet I still wanted him. I still craved him, still thought about him continuously. For some reason I started to think back to those hazy Manchester days, to Alan, and Justin. I remembered the way I had felt with Justin; the miraculous way our relationship had begun among the cherry blossom and the first flakes of pollen.

I wanted to feel that again; the arms and the love of somebody new, the melting of hard resolve into that blissful, dewy surrender. The reaching out for an unobtainable solution. It was one of the worst periods of my life. I have not forgotten the tearful nights, the secret crying, the longing, the guilt. I was miserable but at least I felt. The drive to see Alan was unfathomable to me. I wanted to be alive and I felt dead when I wasn't near to him. I had that sense of need, which I found to be missing from my life as the course progressed. Without need, there can be no fulfilment. Life back then was balanced on the wing of a bird; dangerous and precarious, yet rich and exciting. None of this spiritless time-filling that I was experiencing in Penzance.

My mind wanders back still further to that unrequited period, when the longing was still locked away inside me, still somehow confined within the boundaries of me. Then, eventually, it burst out on some words uttered by his tongue. How strange that when the bird finally flew it was from him and not from me; I felt no tearing of my body as the cage was wrecked, simply that I was surrounded at last by the boundless sky I had been seeking. My feet were suddenly sailing through the blue sky; I barely needed to cling to the neck of the bird. As the white, perfect clouds whizzed around my head, his fingers grasped a few strands of my hair and stroked them with a touch so light that I only felt it by the churning feeling that overtook me. Soon, he took me by the waist and offered our first kiss. I took it, afraid, guilty, cheating, yet the rush of blood through my head and my loins made me take still more. And he gave still more, and I gave too, until we quite nearly fainted with that unique fever of passion at last released.

Things changed after Alan kissed me. I was light-headed; I neglected the parts of myself that were not for Alan. And those that were for him I nurtured more carefully and conscientiously than I ever had. I polished myself for him in a way that I had never considered for Justin. I lost weight, my figure becoming closer by the day to the shape I had always longed to be but never previously had the power to attain. Alan gave me that power. I felt as though it was always spring, as though I could take the old wrecks of my flowers and branches and turn them into something new. Something bright and vital, something that people would breathe in and marvel at. Justin simply did not figure in the equation. Poor, irrelevant Justin. Me-and-Justin had been stale for some time, riding along on a wave of insecurity and faked orgasms. There was no point to me and Justin. Being with him managed to clear the point away from my life, until I felt like a mannequin, one of Joe's figures, but with less life, less energy. Alan took my rough, jaded existence and gave me hope, interest, and a soul. He offered me far more than the love and the sex he meant to offer, and I fed off him and his gifts for many months.

The summer was just beginning when this first kiss blew my life into unfamiliar shapes. They flew up into the air and mingled with the contrails and the summer aeroplanes and the last fragments of blossom that whirled around above our heads. We spent hours walking by the canal, timed so that Justin would not notice, and yet, although he never saw Alan, he knew. I was full of buds, the sap was rising to my head, making me dizzy and radiant. I filled my bathroom with new and exotic shower gels and shampoos. I liked my body for the first time in my life. I would stare at myself in the bath, stroke my own skin, whilst closing my eyes and trying to muster up the sense that it was

Alan. And then I would lift myself out of the bath and twist my body so that I could look in the mirror and see the drops glistening on my slender figure. I made sure the towels were always light and fluffy like whisked eggs. I stroked myself dry before dabbing sticky clouds of white moisturiser all over myself and coaxing my skin to absorb it in ever increasing circles.

This was what I wanted to feel. Cold and alone in my sterile hotel room, I was lost in a dark, dank world of sacrifices. There was no driving force, no surging light to guide me. Even a light in the wrong direction would have been better than this turgid stillness. And with this, I began to impart logical arguments to my sudden lust for someone new. I knew that whenever I have been deeply involved in something, anything, I have run away, that I should curb this habit before I lost Joe too. Ridiculous, but it made sense. I started to feel that maybe fantasy was better than reality, as I had felt just as I started to emerge out of that cocoon of depression after my first few weeks in Peterborough. But most of all, I remembered what I had felt for Alan, and how it was so much more immediate, more urgent, than anything I had ever felt for Joe. Lust is the word; it had been built on no foundation, but our need for each other had been enormous and intense.

I have heard that this kind of intermediate lust can, over time, become love as solid as that built on less slidey foundations. A voice in my head begged me to believe this in those Manchester days when I was trying to work out what to do, but in the end I was not man (or woman) enough to take this risk. And so I fled, from Alan, from Justin, from my home and all that I knew, and found myself once again alone and in the wilderness. Guilt and some form of disgust precluded me from staying with Justin. Alan had been procured dishonestly and could not therefore be kept; my passage was clear.

I could manage without Joe. The thought frightened me. Until now I had thought that I could not exist without him and feared for my sanity should I ever lose him. It is frightening when your life turns around like this and you realise that everything you have believed has been back to front. I had felt some of this when I escaped from Justin and Alan, but at least then I had made a decision of my own. Now what hit me was a cold realisation out of the stark blue. My life had been revolving around what I had taken to be a necessity, but suddenly this was not the case. I still wanted him; I had no wild plans to run off without him and terminate our cohabitation before it had even begun. It was simply the sudden and startling self-knowledge that I did not have to be with him, that life would not end or even be that bad if I was suddenly without him.

I tried not to acknowledge this, in the same way I had earlier tried to ignore those less tangible worms of doubt, but I found this an impossible task. It is difficult to want something intensely and yet wonder if you should take it. I suppose it is a theme that has run through my life, pushing itself to the forefront at various stages. I am still not sure why I left Sheffield and my biology degree. I was enjoying it. I was enthusiastic about both the work and the social life, and I was ecstatic about being away from home. And yet I knew, somehow, that it was something I could not have.

I left Manchester because of Alan and Justin, whom I also left. I could have chosen one of them rather than taking the dramatic step that I did. I could have chosen to stay in Manchester with neither of them but I decided instead to have nothing. Perhaps emptiness is a kind of freedom for me. I have felt that before – the lack of possessions, of ties, of relationships, the ecstasy it can invoke. For most people, destitution would be the worst thing that could happen, but for me it has a kind of a romantic hue. Sometimes the human spirit and the offerings of nature are, or should be, enough.

Trains. Old, smelly underground trains, moleing around beneath the sprawling city. Trains. Training. I suppose there is a relationship between the two words. Training is a kind of preparation for something, and travelling by train is a preliminary to arriving at a destination. Both are prerequisites for the achievement of an end. I sometimes think I have spent my whole life on trains of one sort or another. I cannot listen to 'Another Town, Another Train' without thinking that maybe it was written for me. I am twenty-five years old and I have lived my life divided between six different towns. That is an average of a little more than four years in one place. If I live to be eighty then I will have made my home in twenty different towns. But I lived in London until I was eighteen, and that was not realistically under my control. So the life that I have *chosen* is that of picking up my roots and moving on every (seven years, five places… an average of 0.75 towns per year…) seventeen months, approximately.

Allowing myself the same lifespan, this means I will live in sixty towns. This prospect is not at all appealing. I hope that I shall soon settle in Durham and stay there for a good many years. After all, this is the first place I will really have *lived*, away from my parents, and without the studenty three-year residence expectancy or the desperation of being stuck in the stationariness of transit.

I do not know. I will never know what my history is going to be until I have lived it. That is the problem with history. We look at the past and we think we can force it into whatever shapes we like, but there is always some unknown factor in the equation of future that we cannot foresee. People tend to think that history and future are opposites; they are not, they are the same thing. Future and past may be opposites in one sense but I don't think that history necessarily means only what is behind us. They are the same stuff, arranged in a long chain; the only thing that changes is our vantage point.

Team spirit. I think I have had enough of it crammed into me in the last couple of months to keep me away from colleagues for the rest of my life. We were led out to the beach, to the sandy expanse by the blue-green ocean and there we had to learn how to work together. It was difficult. I wanted to concentrate on breathing in the sunny air, filling my lungs and my heart with the smell and the taste of the seaside, feeling the sand that got into the gaps between my toes no matter what I wore on my feet. I looked out to sea, and at the very edge of the water was the sky. It reminded me of The Fens, although monochrome and a little wetter.

The Fens were once a vast expanse of water, much like the sea. In medieval times, the silt and peat fens were covered with sheep in the summer, but in the winter, or when the rain came down, huge areas became completely waterlogged, flooded by the waters of a plethora of rivers: the Nene, the Cam, the Welland

and the Ouse, the Lark and the Wissey. The landscape must have been very different then to the patchy fields zigzagged by dykes that it is today.

In the fourteenth and fifteenth centuries the local people went out with their spades and their compasses and dug little channels in attempts to make their land cultivable, inhabitable. From the seventeenth century the task was tackled on a much larger scale. The Romans had made attempts at drainage on such a scale, but the first person to tackle it subsequently was Bishop Morton.

From his time onwards, various large straight cuts were made, some of which are still there today, but most of which have been continually altered, or replaced entirely. In 1630 the Dutch, with their experience of dykes and drainage and water control, came and undertook work on an enormous scale. For many years, if you had looked across The Fens, you would have seen thousands of little men digging great channels, altering the landscape for ever.

Here in Penzance, seagulls swooped over the wavering water, dipping down to pick up a fish from time to time. The grey spots on their backs glinted in the sunlight, blown by the wind though they were. Herring gulls, black-headed gulls, black-backed and common ones, kittiwakes. Sometimes some smaller birds joined in, and I could see them hanging from their cliff face homes. I looked across at Bryony and saw that she was watching them too. Every now and then a swooping bird would be reflected in her eyes, doubled in their moist glassy surface, a world where everything existed twice for the perceptive.

The new landscape of The Fens finally emerged. Vermuyden, the Dutch engineer, was given land in return for his work, and The Fens began to be enclosed. Cabbages and cereals were grown and farmsteads were built. The Fens were drained, but this was not the end of the story. Unexpectedly, the level of the land started to fall, particularly in the south, as the peat was sucked dry, became tightly packed and eventually sank, dried out, and sometimes blew away.

A bucket, a spade, various random plastic tools: in teams of four or less build the best and most elaborate sandcastle you can manage in an hour and a half. It was embarrassing and tedious, but we set to work with as much team spirit as we could bear to muster. A pile of sand here, a turret there, a moat perhaps, some odd-shaped, collapsing windows. The beach slowly and quietly – for the sand was soft underfoot and some people had removed their shoes – became a row of inelegant miniature sand homes.

The Fens began to be populated by wind pumps, then steam engines and finally diesel engines in more and more efficient efforts to keep the water off the land. The landscape is still dotted with the buildings that housed such machinery; grand, tall brick buildings that were once the homes of the wind pumps, and smaller and smaller ramshackle sheds as the technology advanced. Today, there are electric pumps that do the same job as the gigantic wind-powered ones.

What was a vast expanse of marshes is now a vast expanse of fields and drains; fields are separated not by hedges, not by fences, but by little rivulets of water that enable people to have their fields and to farm them. The sea might one day reclaim the land, as its level forever rises and it plots to envelop great areas of low-lying flatlands, but for now the land belongs to the farmers and the pheasants and the lapwings. The efforts to abate the water continue; drainage is a continuous process, not something that can be done once and then forgotten about. The cuts and ditches change their courses and are dug and redug as the need arises. Houses and homesteads are built where the ground is suitable, dream homes built on the silt and gravel beds of the old streams, which are more stable than the peat.

Mostly, people built their own dream sand home, their own castles in the air, despite the need to share their abode with their team members, and the results were little, or sometimes enormous, mounds of sand with higgledy-piggledy personalised features scattered about them. I think our supervisors expected this, as they had built something splendid and consistent, and happily pointed out that this was because they were all heading in the same direction. Not, of course, because they had been doing this several times a year for goodness knows how long.

The castle that Bryony and I built was not splendid or grand; in fact it was on quite a small scale, probably because we spent more time talking and giggling and letting the sun fall on our bare heads than we did building. We were quite pleased with it, though, and we took pictures of it – pictures of her, me and it, but never all three together, since one of us had to hold the camera. We didn't win the prize – did I mention that it was a competition? – but I think we were the happiest team on the beach.

You can travel on a train through The Fens today and notice differences in the landscape from day to day. It is a different world when it is dry from when it is flooded, or ploughed, or bursting with plants. You know it is the same place but nothing is familiar. You know you have been here before, but all the colours, all the landmarks, all the reference points are new.

That Friday I spoke to Joe on the phone. It was the first time we had talked for more than a few seconds since my departure for the course, due to his lack of a telephone. We had both been reluctant to spend large amounts of money in payphones, but our separation had reached the stage where we needed to talk for longer, so at a pre-arranged time, he put his expensive phonecard in the slot and dialled my number. I had been standing by the phone for what seemed like hours when I was finally startled by the sharp ringing tones. Sometimes things are more likely to make us jump if we are expecting them; sometimes when we are waiting for a particular sound, we startle at the slightest twitch of a whisker.

'Hello?'

'Angel!'

There was an expensive pause as we both tried to think of how to fit in all the things we wanted to say. Eventually Joe settled for, 'How are you getting on?'

'Oh, okay. Not too bad, I suppose.'

'Is it really *that* bad?' I could hear a smile at his mouthpiece.

'Just boring and pointless, I suppose.'

I tried to bring myself to describe some of our activities, but this was surprisingly difficult. In my musings, I had given my memory of him a different hue to reality, and he felt like a stranger.

'How about you?' I dropped into the silence. 'What have you been up to? How's work?'

'Same as usual really. I've done quite a bit with the house, though.'

I suppressed a 'Don't do anything too drastic without me!' – I knew he wouldn't. As men go, Joe was actually a fairly sensitive one. I suppose that was why I loved him so much. And yes, I did love him. But somehow when I thought about making love with him, it was difficult to imagine. It had been too long. I felt like I had grown away from him. The thought of sex with him seemed actually disgusting. I hoped that this was not detectable in my voice, as we continued to talk of mutually uninteresting things. I wondered if this was what all relationships degenerated into if given long enough, hoping that this was not the case, but feeling suddenly unoptimistic.

I remember now a later conversation I had with Bryony about Joe. She caught me looking glum, just a few days before I saw her for the last time. She walked over to me and placed a hand on my shoulder. I had been so engrossed in my reverie that I had not noticed her approaching, and her touch made me shiver. I felt as though I would jump out of my skin, but some unknown source of self-control made me still. My sudden shiver metamorphosed into a long, slow sliver that slid down my back and radiated out through my limbs. Her realisation of this came as though I had shocked her, sent electricity surging through her veins, and she was thrown back.

'I'm sorry, I didn't mean to startle you.'

I turned my head to face her and gave her as controlled a smile as I could manage. 'Don't worry. I was miles away.'

She seated herself next to me and poured herself a cup of the thick brown liquid that had been nestling at the bottom of the teapot, too polite or too intent on something or other to comment.

'What's going on in that head of yours?' she enquired playfully, gently tousling my hair with one hand while the other worked the spoon in concentrated circles through her tea. It was as though she could weaken it if she worked hard enough.

She knew me well enough by now to tell if I lied about my thoughts, and I did not have the energy to try to convince her of anything but the truth. Sighing slightly, I admitted something to her that I was still only on the verge of acknowledging to myself. 'I think I might leave Joe.'

I could tell from her face that she was aghast, but her voice was calm. 'Why? You two are so in love. I could tell right from the word go.'

I sighed again. 'At the word go we were in love. Something has happened to me. I don't know what. I am too far apart from him now.'

She was silent, as though she knew all too well what it was that had happened to me, and I was aware of her avoiding meeting my eyes, as I was hers.

Somehow, in the few days between my telephone conversation with Joe and my confidence in Bryony, something had happened. A process that had begun slowly and subtly had cartwheeled out of its steady orbit and was whirling about, out of control, blowing me with it in its slipstream. I was still desperately in love with Joe, I knew that I was, but there was some primeval voice inside me telling me that this was the beginning of the end, that I had to let go now before it was too late.

We have stopped at some indeterminate place beneath London, as these tube trains sometimes do in an effort to terrify their passengers. I try to look out of the windows but there is only darkness out there. I know that the walls enclose the train tightly and closely but I cannot see them. Now I cannot imagine not wanting Joe. I have travelled a full circle and he need never know. If my love for Joe was a pond, the ripples had grown too far apart, just as Joe and I were geographically apart. I mistook the calm between those ripples for the whole skin of the pond; flat and smooth and lifeless. I sigh. What of the superimposed circles I found in Alan and Justin? Two pebbles (like the pebbles I threw into the sea with Bryony) violating the same pond, so I chose not to wait and see which ripple expired first, nor to put a sustaining effort into one; no, I chose to turn my back on the pond. I decided that I was not the pond after all and I could walk away. So I ran.

I almost ran from Penzance. The running would not have been anything particularly new, but this time I felt different. I was almost through it, almost there. I had done most of the hard bits.

All I had to do was sit it out and then at the end take the things I had always wanted as payment. Yet I almost couldn't do it. It all seemed so futile, so pointless. How could I not consider running away? From the course, and from Joe as well, perhaps. I think that one of the things that made me resist the impulse to repeat history and fly as far as I could from the life I was in was the fact that I had done it before, but Bryony was also an aid in restraint. She pointed out to me what a stupid mistake I would be making; she acted as an emotional jailer. Perhaps my life would have turned out very differently had I met her when I was nineteen.

'I can't do this, you know,' I said out of my hair which I had let drape over my face in a lethargic stoop.

She looked up from the button she was sewing on to her coat. 'What?'

I realised I was thinking aloud, that I hadn't meant to say anything.

'I don't know,' I said, my thoughts flowing from my mouth almost without the middle level of consciously forming them into words. 'Joe, this job, the whole package. I don't know what I'm doing here.'

She moved closer to me and laid a comforting hand on my arm. For some reason, my skin scorched beneath her touch.

'Why not? What's happened to you?'

I didn't know the answer to this. I am closer to this answer now, but even if I had known it then, I don't think I would have been able to tell her. Perhaps she already knew.

'What is the alternative?' she asked, frustratingly logical.

I was silent.

'Well, doesn't that answer your dilemma?'

I thought about how I had chosen nothing over something in the past, and I thought about saying that it didn't necessarily, but I held my tongue.

'Seriously,' she pressed, 'what are you going to do? Give up the course and the job? Give up Joe? Where would you go? What would you do? In a few weeks' time when this course is over you will be sitting in some hovel somewhere knowing that if you had stuck it out it would all be over.'

She was right, of course. And I had sat alone in a hovel before.

I had no desire to repeat the experience. I suppose she had an ulterior motive. If I left, she would be alone and friendless in Penzance, in the same way that I was after she had gone. Our friendship was new, and I too was loath to splinter it in its vital early stages. Staying there would allow us to nurture it and to have fun and help each other through the course at the same time. I think we both wanted something more from each other than we felt we were supposed to, even from the beginning, when we nestled on the sofa together that first evening. Even though we didn't speak, I think we both began to know each other then. Perhaps that is why we didn't speak. I didn't feel myself to be very absorbed in her at the time but I think beneath my corporate exterior I was.

We try to label everyone we meet; we try to understand them by the compartments we put them in. But somehow we rarely see past to the heart within.

Isn't love what really matters? Isn't that what we humans are doing here? Loving each other, the sky and the stars and the trees and the water and our pet cats and our wallpaper? The human soul has an enormous capacity for enjoyment, and it is this that should be nurtured, not the artificial morals and the social dogmas that make us the nervous, tortured people we have become. It is love that gives us the wings to soar above the tower blocks that we work in and the concrete boxes that we live in, to take ourselves away from everything that doesn't matter. The things that matter most to an individual are usually the things that matter least to society. If I can feel love, then I want to feel it, and I don't care whether it is for a woman or a man, a work of art or music, a poem or a hamster. I want to feel the love. Everyone wants to love and be loved.

*

The little girl gets to her feet and runs into the house. She checks the places where she thinks she would like to sleep if she had been born a kitten: the sofa; the big, soft bed where her parents sleep; the rug in front of the fire. She does not find it in any of these places. She asks her brothers for a clue, but all they will say is, 'You are very cold.' She recognises this as the colder–warmer game that she has often played with them. She realises that if she grits her teeth and follows their instructions she will find her cat, and this is what she does.

She walks towards the kitchen. Daniel tells her that she is very cold. She changes direction and walks towards the living room once more. Warmer now, she hears, so she continues in her tracks. But then she is colder again, and she does not know what to do. The only thing that lies between the kitchen and the living room is the little blue door that leads out into the narrow passage at the side of the house, so she opens this and walks out. The passage is dark, and smells dank and musty, and she is frightened. She has only been into the house this way with her father a few times, when she has helped him in the garden. The passage leads to the wooden shed where father keeps his tools and a lot of boxes full of all sorts of things. She knows that this is kept locked, so they must have hidden her cat somewhere near the front of the house.

★

Perhaps I would leave Joe. I was not sure at this point. I think I believed it would not happen immediately but it would happen. It felt like a matter of sitting on the water-filled balloon and waiting for the constant strain of my weight to finally become too much for it and burst it. There did not seem to be any other way. I would go back home, to Durham, try to pretend that everything was as it should be, but in my private moments I would continually be examining whether or not the time was right to make my move. I supposed I would stop loving Joe in time, in much the same way that the husbands and wives in arranged marriages grow to love each other if they are prepared to let this happen.

Then what would I do? I would flounder on with my life, perhaps alone for the rest of it, perhaps falling in and out of relationships with people whom I may or may not be in love with, but in either case would not be capable of sustaining anything long term with. There are a lot of things that one can do in solitude that are impossible when there is a partner waiting in the wings. I could travel. I didn't want to but the option would be there. I could go to Egypt. I could spend my time doing the things I wanted to do and not have to make compromises so that

I could be together with my partner often enough for the relationship to begin to crumble. Peterborough had been fun in its own way, despite the depression and the struggle. Although I did not really want to do any of the things that single people do, I felt I would like to have the opportunity and the freedom, just in case I should one day want to.

Bryony could sprout wings whenever she chose. There was no one tied to her by means of an invisible umbilical cord, no heart that was supposed to beat simultaneously with hers. The nights were not lonely for her – she had her own company, her own good nature. I could not believe that a woman like her could ever want for anything, since she could never be without herself. What it must be to live constantly with perfection! For I did think that Bryony was perfect. I realise that now, more than ever. And how fragile perfection is; how easily it can be broken. China plates are nearer to perfection than plastic ones (neither of course being in particularly close proximity to this ultimate quality). A china plate will smash when dropped on to a spongy surface, while its cheaper cousins bounce unharmed from concrete floors. Perhaps china is more valued because of its very fragility; and yet I did not think of Bryony as fragile. She was porcelain and delicate in the most appealing of ways, but it was clear that she inwardly possessed the strength of a hundred crates of plastic kitchenware.

But what is strength? You could build an enclosure and make it everything-proof so that nothing from outside could harm its contents. You could make it impossible for anything to get in, but if you didn't realise that the real danger was posed by the things that were already inside, your efforts would all have been in vain.

Bryony

London. I have traversed it, and now I sit at King's Cross, this vast, fragile station. Looking up at the ceilings I see that they are made of gossamer, of butterflies' wings. The station seems so old that the slightest gust of wind might collapse it like a card house, sending hearts and diamonds, clubs and spades, falling, twisting, red, white and black, showering down on the ant-like people roaming the concourse. No one spared; kings, queens and jacks alike, twirling to the ground with aces to tens.

It is difficult to believe that London was ever my home. So much has passed since then. The little house in Putney saw and indeed created many of my defining experiences. Yet I have left it behind, open-mouthed, gaping, now accommodating only my parents, bereft of the noise and spirit of children. When I left Sheffield, ashamed and embarrassed for my parents' sake, and yet for my own mind relieved, we drove down to London, the Fiesta bulging with my adolescent possessions. Yorkshire had seemed so big, so empty after the vomit-ridden reaches of London, and I was sorry in some small way to be leaving it behind. I had been home for Christmas, but that had been a holiday, whereas now I was giving up all I had attained and progressing backwards – regressing. I tried to muster up some excitement: Oxford Street; the huge, musty smell of the parks; the great, snaking river that dominated all our lives. It was no good. Rugged hillsides, sparkling new trams and Meadowhall had become my life, in the space of a few months.

I have plenty of time before my train arrives, and I wander around the old station. Like Paddington, it is a Grade I listed building. I suppose this is inevitable, yet it is strange that a station still in use should hold such historic importance. Isn't history something that is past, gone, finished? How can it coexist with everyday life? I remember reading that King's Cross is going to be restored at some point in the future: the shed roofs, the footbridge and platforms. It is also going to be redecorated. In a way this is a shame. The dirt, the grime of London, seems so right here, and I cannot imagine the place without it. The clock tower has already begun to be reconditioned and is covered in scaffolding and small orange men with yellow stripes across their backs. It is dark and gloomy in here, the way railway stations should be, but they are going to improve the lighting. They are also going to put in more shops.

Bryony lives in Godalming – lived in Godalming, I remind myself. A province of Guildford, in turn one of those sprawling backwater districts of London, separated by it as the United Kingdom from the rest of Europe by some ancient sliding of geography, or perhaps of sociology. She told me about the vast reaches of the Hog's back, the view from its beginning as far as Canary Wharf, seen through the brown-grey mist when conditions were right. She described the way it crept into Hampshire, brown in the autumn, white with snow in winter, then yellow with buttercups and daisies and violent green for the spring, whetting my appetite. She invited me to visit her and see it for myself, and I told her that I would, and meant it – not like so many similar conversations I have had with friends whom I never saw again. I will go there. It will be almost a pilgrimage for me now. I cannot follow Bryony forward but I can go back into her life, her history, to the things that were important to her, to the place she loved so deeply.

Hands, enclosing my waist, and a soft, musical voice close to me. A woman's voice, and a woman's lips breathing out words into my ear, her breath on the surrounding skin. I feel the sensation of Bryony whispering to me, whispering her secrets, and smile slightly to myself. But the image changes; now she is lying on a carpeted floor, the *chink* and rattle of glasses and voices going on around her, her breath failing, her sweet, sweet breath, spent and fading. I jerk my head to one side in a vicious attempt to erase the image from my brain. It is one that I have invented in my own perverse mind, that has never existed but in this mass of brain tissue squirming around inside my head. Yet I am unable to chase it away.

The photographs were good. There was nothing artistic about

them but they had captured enough of Penzance to satisfy me. After I picked them up from Boots, I ran to Bryony's room to share them with her. It had been so long since I started the film that I could not remember what was on it. The first few pictures were of Joe, me and Joe, the exterior of our new house. There were even a couple of sad pictures of Nottingham things at the very beginning, taken with the poignant air of consciously creating a memoir.

'Is this him, then?' she grinned, taking the first picture of him as close to her face as she could and scrutinising it. She knew the answer.

'Yes. What do you think?' I teased, slightly uneasily. She said that he looked as wonderful as my descriptions of him, and that she was jealous. I dismissed the thought, 'Of whom?' I knew that she was not, that she preferred to be alone, that she preferred her wings to be spread out alongside her rather than tied behind her back. I started to pick through the rest of the photographs.

'Oh, this is me and Evelyn in Cripps Hall. That's the door to my room.'

'Nice door,' she said with a grin. The pictures of Penzance began then. There was a grim shot of the hotel on the first evening, before I had ever seen Bryony, the view from the window of my room – the usual things. There were a few pictures of our sandcastle. We laughed. In the first there was the sandcastle and Bryony, and in the second I was there instead, on the other side of the construction.

'Look! You could put them together and see us both with it,' she giggled, following her own instructions. She overlapped the two pictures of the castle, and sure enough, there was a picture of a sandcastle with Bryony and me sitting one each side of it.

I wonder, fighting for a space to sit in this huge terminal, whether I should be hiding my grief. I wonder also whether I should be feeling it. It has been almost a month now, and I am going home, to my new life, to the place where I have longed to be for a very long time. Yet still I cannot shake off this cloud. The people around me are mostly sporting blank faces. Some of them are in groups, laughing and joking together. I still wonder how they find the strength to be happy, even now, even so long after those dark weeks in Peterborough. What is there to smile about, even when things are going comparatively well?

I sigh quietly to myself. It must be a show. Unless I am different to the rest of them, it must be artificial. They leave their cosy, dark hideaways in the morning and come to stand out in the open, the closet doors closed firmly behind them by an effort of will and determination. But at night, away from the compulsions of company, they retreat back into the cupboards where they store all their sadness and misery, supping on it, inhaling it, steeling themselves for another faceless, emotion-free tomorrow. It is like taking a fix, like the painful prick of a needle, when the bruises are felt and the skin is pierced, followed by the wait for temporary bliss. Surely we are all closet depressives, and only a few of us dare to come out.

I once took a train from the shady familiarity of home to Embankment Station and walked purposefully out on to Hungerford Bridge. I stared out over the black, oily water as the bridge shook with the weight and the friction of the trains that hulked along, vast and alone, behind the almost ornate piece of iron between me and them. The golden dome of St Paul's glittered at me from the distance, and to my right the lights of the South Bank beckoned me. Once, when my viola playing had been a lot worse and my expectations of the standard I would reach a lot better, I had entertained notions of performing there, as a soloist. The thick lighting of the stage shining down around me, the boards beneath me forming my own space. My bow would travel the strings, now softly, now authoritatively. My harmonics would soar without a hint of scratching, and my pizzicato would be short and plucky and richly thin. I stood for an hour on that bridge, not afraid of the tramps and the drunkards as I would be now, not ruffled by the cold wind nor afraid of falling into and being enveloped by the beautiful yet poisonous waters below me. This image of London is not consistent with the others I have. It seemed, for that infinitesimally small part of my life, a beautiful place, a grand place, and I felt, for once, that it could bring me fulfilment. Then I left home for Sheffield and knew for the first time what it was like to be free.

London makes some people stand tall; for them, it is an

uplifting, cosmopolitan place, filled with life, with vigour. Such people know that underneath the grimy grey there is bright inspiration; they can peel off the dull surface and reveal strips of flashing colours beneath that spur them on to do new and great things. Famous, glittering people live in London. It is the necessary centre to the lives of so many people.

This is not how London makes me feel. It makes me small and helpless, as I hunch my back and follow the crowds of unfeeling zombies through the underground tunnels. There is no way to go but with the momentum; you have to walk at their pace, and it does not change. London reminds me that there are too many people in the world. Is it the fault of the road builders, the public transport bosses, that the roads are so full and the trains and buses so repugnant with people? Sometimes I feel frustrated with transport authorities. Why don't they make it better? But every now and then, I come to London and I know what the problem really is. Now I feel that horror – the horror of the knowledge that the world is brimming full of people, more people than it can hold. No road system will ever be adequate. We could turn the whole anvil-shape of this island into one big piece of concrete with criss-crossed white lines and endless lanes, and still it would be overcrowded with people trying to travel somewhere. No room for those who wanted to stay still.

I can feel everyone travelling around me. When you stand in London, there are people journeying all around you, above your head in aeroplanes, below your feet in the dark maze of the underground. People surrounding you on all sides and in every dimension, much the same as the trees in my childhood nightmares. The trees, at least, were only present in my sleeping hours and were not real. The people, the journeys, are always there, always clamouring, always roots and tendrils, trunks and long ugly branches, sucking me into their world, closing me in.

I think of olden times. It is said that there are more people alive now than have ever died. This frightens me. I wonder exactly when this period of people dying is supposed to have started – in the year nought? At some arbitrary stage of evolution where it is deemed we can be called 'man'? It does not matter. Since the growth is exponential, whichever point we choose the answer will be the same: there will always be more people alive than have died.

The swarms of people that history reports at various significant events were not as huge as the numbers of people we see every day in these modern times. A hundred years ago, two hundred, the world must have been empty, full of vast plains of desolation. Yet now it is more desolate. Everywhere there are rivers, seas of people, mighty oceans of human life, and in the flux each one of us becomes more anonymous and less significant. The world used to be a huge forest to be explored and conquered. Robin Hood's Sherwood was many times bigger than it is now, yet more people live today in a small area of what was the forest than lived in the entire tree-ridden state then.

I think it might be nice to live on the moon. To live in a new, lunar society, to move through the sky with Diana, hunter of the clouds, to spend my life in a silvery Phoebean luxury. When they discovered water there the whole idea of a colony of humans living on the moon rose up afresh. It is so distant, so mysterious, and so unpopulated. I think it must be like this planet was before civilisation. There are many differences, but the similarity is in its virginity. What must the first Earth people have thought of their habitat? No doubt they thought nothing of it, but imagine going back to that now. The emptiness preceding Mesopotamia, Babylon. To create cities from nothing. To create empires and cultures, indeed Culture. To work the bare planet into one's own designs and fancies. There would be a lot of space on the moon, a lot of open sky and stars and clouds.

Of course, this is fantasy. There is not enough oxygen on the moon. There is not enough gravity on the moon. We would have to live in specially constructed enclosed spaces, which would never be vast and empty in the way that I imagine. But it is compelling sometimes to look there and wonder. The moon, measurer of time, clock of the sky, the heavens, and of biological systems. Does time pass when you are on the hands of the clock? Could I live my life there in an eerie timelessness? Would my history be the same as my future, my present, all bathed equally in the same starry glitter?

I remember looking at the moon and the stars with Bryony.

The moment was so beautiful and so intense that I took her hand in mine, and she did not mind. I think that was the moment our real fusion began. Being there and being in contact with the night sky all around us, darting in between our fingers and through our hair, caused us to melt into one another. Her hand was small and warm, and I held it gently but proudly – a prized possession. Our palms were pressed flatly together, but I could feel the electricity of the night flowing between them, the moonbeams dancing nymph-like over and under our fingernails, our knuckles. I am on a station. I look around me and feel startled to have immersed myself in this moment here, among all these anonymous and abstract people. No one on this vast station knows anything of Bryony. None would care if they did. The spiky tears start to prick at my eyes.

Sometimes when I wake up in the morning and the sun is bursting its way through the curtains in long sharp rays, I become sad. It makes me feel as though I am living every experience in my life at once. My head becomes filled with a light and airy freshness that blows through my brain and sings to me of past achievements and sorrows. Sometimes on such mornings this feeling is so strong that I do not know where I am, and all I can do is lie in bed and wait until the crossbeams of different parts of my life have finished their spidery crawl over me.

It was like this on that bright morning when I awoke in the hotel room and realised I wasn't alone. The curtains shot out at me and dragged my eyes into the mazy pattern printed on them. I was stuck in a dream that waking could not get me out of, until suddenly reality squirted into my head and I recognised my surroundings. So far, the days had been mostly dull and indistinguishable from one another, and I was glad for a sunny one. Then something stirred at my feet, and my breathing instantly postponed itself. I wondered if I was still asleep, or drunk, or gone mad, but a fraction of a second later I realised what was happening.

I didn't remember going to bed last night, but then I suppose I hadn't really. A corner of the duvet was lying nonchalantly over my leg, but I was fully clothed and my head was not on my pillow. I lifted my head and looked at Bryony. She was very close to me, curled up on the end of the bed, facing out at the window. The thin material on her back undulated slightly with the rhythm of her breathing, and her hair lay spread out behind her.

I wondered how she was doing this to me. Looking at her sent shivery worms sliding through my stomach. I felt a vague panic, although I knew we had done nothing but collapse on the bed together when it got late. I looked at the wine bottles on the dressing table, two empty and one containing a small amount of golden liquid, and wondered why I didn't remember drinking so much.

I was with Bryony for a very short time but it feels to me as though I experienced her in every part of my life, just like the sunbeams that caressed us both on that morning. She was many things to me but this is how I will remember her. I could have reached out and touched her. I could have stroked her soft hair. I could have laid my unworthy fingers on her skin and known what it felt like to touch her, known what the surface of her skin was like beneath my fingers. She was small and fragile there on my bed but big enough to fill the whole room with herself and to wholly envelop me in her. For a long time I could only stare at her, while making a desperate effort to control my breathing, and wonder whether I should wake her. It was after nine, and we should have been well into the day's activities by now, but somehow I knew we would be taking the day off.

The previous day had been a tough one. We had been told to wear something that we didn't mind ruining and led out into a field that they had filled with wooden obstacles and huge vats of water. We were put forcibly into teams of two with random fellow trainees and expected to form an instant coalition with them in order to complete various tasks in less time than the other pairs. I didn't do too badly. I was coupled with a timid-looking woman who seemed to have no problem-solving skills of her own and was happy for me to take charge of her and force on to her my own pathetic attempts at solutions.

Bryony's partner was a middle-aged man with a huge midriff and an ego to match, whose philosophy seemed to be that since she was a young woman and he an old man, she would be delighted to do as he instructed. I saw her from time to time protesting, but he seemed to be one of those men who wouldn't listen to his inferiors – as he clearly saw her – no matter how intelligent the things they had to say. He crushed her, I could tell. She was not timid, nor arrogant, and she coped, but I saw her spirit fading with each moment that passed.

To make it worse, when they failed at almost every task and came even lower down the scheme than my puny assistant and me, her partner had the nerve to stand up in front of everyone and say in no uncertain terms that it was her fault; that he would have performed better with a more able person on his team and that she had been not only unable but also unwilling to throw herself into the spirit of the event.

I knew that Bryony had been humiliated by these things, and I wanted to console her, to lift her spirits, with some vague premonition of the feeling that didn't really consolidate in me until I woke up to find her beside me. I skipped dinner – which must explain why when I drank it was so sweet and sickly and potent – and bought the wine and the chocolate. Then I knocked on Bryony's door and found her lethargic and thin spirited. She said that her head was aching – not exactly a headache but an aching head – and that she was exhausted, no doubt from the day's exertions.

I could tell that she had been crying, too; the marks on her face attested that she had spent some time in this activity, but I could also tell that she would prefer me not to point this out. For some reason, the opening of Beethoven's Seventh Symphony burst into my head and the air was like the lyrical meandering of the tune, punctuated by our occasional speech. I thought I might have difficulty in persuading her to leave her solitude, but she seemed pleased that I had gone to find her, and we went along the corridor to my room.

We started on the wine. I waited for the pink-red liquid to have an effect on her. She was worn, tense; I wanted to make her relax. Little was said. I think she was happy to have someone with her, and I was happy to be with her. Time slid by, slowly. I don't know if she knew that my eyes rested on her almost continually. I wanted to make sure that the wine was making her feel better and not worse. I wanted to look with my eyes into the thoughts in her head, into her distress, and lift it out of her. I didn't want to take my eyes off her.

'Do you mind if I listen to some music?' I eventually asked, my hand reaching into the pocket of my suitcase ready to pull out the cheap portable CD player. Hearing the Beethoven in my head had made me urgent to listen to it.

'No, I don't mind.'

I remembered her headache. 'Are you sure? Your head's okay?'

'Yes, my head will be fine.'

I began to rummage around for the CD. 'Beethoven, Seventh Symphony?' I asked.

She nodded.

I inserted the disc into the machine and pressed the play button.

Some people think that home listening is a question of expensive hi-fi equipment. The more they spend, the better the music will be. They think it is a case of frequencies and wavelengths being pushed through various tubes and filters and wires, and that it is the equipment that does all the work, not the music. Beethoven would have been horrified. It is true that there are some mediocre pieces that are transformed into something magical by a good performance or a shiny CD shoved into a monstrous player, but music such as the Beethoven needs no aid. The tones leap out into the air, independently of the electronics. They dance around ears and bodies and faces and they work the composer's magic.

I opened the second bottle of wine just as the second movement was beginning. She smiled languidly at me and held out her glass, into which I poured the thick, red liquid. I filled my own glass too, and we relaxed into the music. The air all around us, like the sound of Beethoven's strings, was rich and dark. We breathed, we sighed, and we let the music into us. I remembered my other purchases and smiled broadly at Bryony.

'I think we need something stronger,' I explained in response to her enquiring look. Her face remained blank, and I went to a cupboard and took out the chocolate. I arranged it in front of us in a geometric pile, ritually, and for a moment we just stared at it, sitting cross-legged on the bed opposite each other, almost afraid to partake of such a great luxury. There is something sacred about chocolate. Quetzalcoatl, the chief god of the Aztecs and the Toltecs, is said to have created it as a gift to his people in the form of a drink, an aphrodisiac, named xocolatl. I pictured the lips opening in the brown faces of these primitive people, their dark eyes shining as the taste flowed into their mouths and their throats. Its predominant form may have changed but not its effect.

The marks of tears still stained the skin around her eyes as I saw the comfort of the chocolate begin to work its magic on her. Her brow creased into the furrowed pattern of thought and imminent speech, and she said, 'You know, you'd be an idiot to leave Joe.'

It was a casual remark but I felt it was heavy with meaning. Was she testing me? Was she concerned about my future, about both our futures? Perhaps I only imagined the added value in that small sentence.

'I suppose you're right.' I sighed a little. I was not sure I wanted her to be right.

'It's frightening what being away from someone can do. It seems either to draw people closer together or to push them far apart. There doesn't seem to be any middle ground.'

'You have experience of this?' I teased, suddenly needing to lighten the atmosphere.

'No, I suppose I just notice things about people. Maybe it's because there's something lacking in my own life or something.'

I ventured to put another piece of chocolate into her mouth for her, since her hands had placed themselves on my arm affectionately. I recognised with a faint shock that I had not noticed her putting them there. She showed no signs of unease, so I popped it in and her lips closed around it. I was a little slow in withdrawing my fingers, and she almost enveloped them too in the black hole of her mouth. I thought I felt the pressure of her lips closing around me, almost that I felt them without touching them.

'Excuse me. Which one of us is the counsellor?' I threw at her.

Cortés brought the rich, dark substance to Europe in the

sixteenth century, where it quickly became a luxury that the upper classes regularly indulged in. They believed it to be a source of wisdom, sexuality and good health. There is some evidence that many became addicted to it. Casanova's love potions were as often made of chocolate as of champagne. It has been praised endlessly as the centuries have progressed; one of the few things that has never gone out of fashion.

'Seriously,' she continued, the chunk now melted and travelling languidly down her throat, 'at least wait until you get home and see how you feel before you make any decisions. This is a weird couple of months. It's not surprising you're feeling a bit low.'

'I'm not feeling low, though,' I contradicted. I wasn't lying. 'I just feel like I don't need him any more, don't want him any more.' I was frightened by just how little this idea upset me, and although I didn't confide this, I think she knew.

'He sounds like a wonderful man. When you're as happy with someone as you obviously are with him, you don't just throw it away.' She paused. 'You know, you haven't said a bad word about him since we met. I think you love him more than you realise.'

I was silent. Again, perhaps she was right. And as she had intimated, I didn't really have anything to lose. And yet I felt the fringe of some strange, unidentifiable emotion pass over me as this thought settled in my head. Did I have anything to lose? I didn't know.

There is another side to chocolate – the sensual side. I thought about this as the wings of the oboe soared the graceful melody over our heads. It was terribly decadent to pluck a piece of chocolate from the voluptuous purple foil of the packet, place it in one's mouth and let it melt into the taste buds, the throat, the digestive system. The air became fuller and richer as the second movement came and went over us. It might have been because of the wine, or it could have been the understanding that was created between us, that funnelled out of the air and hung around us, warm and comforting. The dance of the third movement stripped us of our reverieic mood, light and dramatic all at once – joyful, yet deeply serious, twirling around our heads like will-o'-the-wisp one moment, then gaining gravity and landing authoritatively on the ground with its sensible blocks of sound and long string notes for stability.

I once went to a concert where the orchestra sat firmly up in their seats and played the last movement at such a startling, fiery speed that the audience too were pulled up in their seats and carried along with the whirlwind. It knocked me out: I walked out into the darkening day when it had finished, encased in a daze. There was some yellow of the sun left behind the dome of the Royal Albert Hall, and London seemed to have stopped under my gaze. After that, the world moved more slowly for several days. This evening I was becoming intoxicated with the wine, which in turn made me less resistant to the intoxication of Bryony, and everything seemed to fall away, slowly, silently, in much the same way.

The further around the clock the little hand moved, the less I can remember. The image, a vision, of Bryony in front of me becomes fuzzy and hazy, although I know she is still there, omnipresent, for ever there. Oh, Bryony, I want to take you in my arms and feel your skin, warm and vibrant against me. I want to make your cold limbs alive again and tangle them around me, to feel your shiny hair on my neck. I want to feel your kisses. The air from your mouth warm and comforting on my cheeks, the moisture from inside forming itself on my lips, exchanging the fluids of our finally entwined souls. I see it as it would be in a movie, our faces moving slowly closer, our lips tantalisingly balancing for an infinite moment on the edge of contact. Then we are pulled together, our tongues and facial muscles making wormy patterns around our mouths. I want to feel the inside of your mouth, its texture, its curvature. You would be soft, softer than a man. I know what the inside of a woman's mouth feels like; all I have to do is run my tongue around the inside of my own cheeks. I can do that anywhere, I can do it now. And yet as I know more about you, everything about how you would feel to touch, I know less, far less than I know about anything.

With the fourth movement of the Beethoven making twisty knots out of my guts and Bryony's all-pervasiveness pulling me still further out of myself, I had no chance at self-control. I had managed until the moment the witty previous movement had darkened and repeated a fragment of itself minorly before its definite closing cadence. Then I had been startled, as always, by the unending of that cadence provided by the opening of the new movement. My concentration was gone and my restraint too to some extent. This was when I closed my eyes and let myself flop on to the bed. I did not expect to sleep. I thought that my brain was too open and awake to allow me to switch off.

Bryony was ripping me in half. I could feel every flake of her soft skin, every point of light in her eyes, every last wisp of her breath. She filled the room, she filled my senses, and she tore at my insides in a way that I cannot begin to explain. The last movement of the Beethoven was still electrifying my nerves and my bones, and I felt more awake and alive and receptive than I ever remember being. The next thing I knew was the light on my face in the morning.

It is difficult to remember the day that followed. I know that I had more fun than I realise. I know that I am feeling a kind of selective amnesia about it, some kind of blocking out, and I know that Freud would have been delighted with me. I have seen similar cases in my psychology textbooks. The traumatic experience pushed to the back of the mind, to somewhere it cannot get out from. A detention, from which it cannot have any influence on the future – or so the unconscious mind thinks. But it is wrong, Freud attests. Such repressed memories have a huge effect on the future, but because they remain unknown, the cause of any resulting psychosis is not clear, and the problem is worsened.

I can picture myself in the analysis chair, Sigmund himself before me, his wild beard framing the bottom half of his face. The words, 'Tell me about your childhood,' spring from his lips, and I laugh. It is not my childhood but my recent past that is inhibited; that, if Freud is right, will prevent me from living my life healthily and happily.

The final outrageous dance of the Beethoven ends as suddenly and definitively as Bryony's life. She should only have been gone for a few minutes. I don't remember much about the rest of that evening either, but I do remember the little window around the catastrophe. I remember it like a curse – it recurs in my nightmares, yet with more and more increasingly horrible variations, and it won't go away.

She decided we needed more wine. I know that we had spent the day as naughty children, dashing in and out of the waves on the beach, running along the sand, hands linked, sometimes wrestling each other to the floor with bright, watery laughter, covering ourselves and each other in the grainy sand. Although it was cold, we didn't care. The sun was shining and we wanted to be bright and adventurous and rebellious. The day had drawn to a close like the last movement of op. 92: storm clouds and low rumbling bass lines and twirly-whirly happiness. Back in the hotel, in her room this time, we didn't want the day to be ended. We had not left each other's sides for the last twenty-four hours, and I think she was as loath as I was to end it here. There had been wine and chocolate again, and also Beethoven, drawing out the evening, lengthening our being together.

It isn't as though we needed the wine. We were drunk with our happiness and each other's spirits, and the last time I saw her alive, her face was set into a wild smile. She started to walk out of the door, and then, for a reason I have not been able to identify, turned and flung her arms around me. I don't remember how that made me feel – I think remembering would be suicidal in terms of my already battered sanity – but I can make a guess.

Why should I have to guess at how I felt in the last moments of her life? I know how I would have felt had I known they were her last. I would have hugged her to me, and cried huge, salty tears all over her, and screamed at her not to leave me. I would have clung to her as though I felt that would prevent her from being torn away from me. I would not have been able to bear it.

Wagner attested this fourth movement to be 'the very apotheosis of the dance'; just as, for me, Bryony was the apotheosis of woman. The fourth movement was for Wagner a dance of spheres personified, a dance in which the rhythm-skeleton is filled out with the firm human figures of melody and harmony. The final embrace of the dance ends in a kiss.

Bryony's firm human figure was beside me as the dance proceeded, her supple body still, her presence nevertheless wafting a dance into my veins. We neither embraced nor kissed; the shape of her body was forever outside my grasp. How I would have loved to sweep her off the bed and on to the floor, join her body with mine in the glorious dance, creating infinitely beautiful movements in the fusion of our bodies, in the art of our dancing. The shapes we made would be now small, now expansive; now still, now filled with graceful movement. Our bodies would arch together, push apart, twirl round and round in crazy circles, fall to the floor in a drop of exhaustion after the heady dance, but we would not feel dizzy or spent. I could have taken her up and danced through my life with her, made both our existences into an art that would know no bounds. I didn't know that the final embrace would come so soon.

Those dreadful few minutes I remember in every detail. I can hardly believe it all fitted into the small amount of time I know it to have done. It was a couple of minutes to nine o'clock. I was starting to twiddle my thumbs. I noticed a black smudge beneath the nail on my left index finger, and poked at it with a small piece of stiff wire I had found somewhere. She should have been back by now. There was a blackbird singing its evening lullaby outside the window, in that distinctive warbling, almost tonal manner. It echoed through the impending darkness, and I closed my eyes at the sweetness of the song. I wondered where else she would go. Maybe she had decided to surprise me with some food. I was certainly hungry. I thought of the foil containers of the Chinese takeaway; chicken in black bean and chilli sauce, prawn crackers, spring rolls, and at the effort a rumble emanated from somewhere below my rib cage. Still, I was worried.

I heard footsteps in the corridor. They finished shuffling up the stairs and dragged along the carpeted floor outside, closer and closer to the door. I thought that it might be Bryony, but then I came to my senses and acknowledged several pairs of feet. Out of the corner of my eye I saw the elaborate edging of the melamine around the mirror, and reflected in the mirror itself was the over-bed lamp on the opposite side of the room. The footsteps outside were accompanied by hushed voices, none of them Bryony's. Then I heard the tinkling of a key chain and someone scrabbling to find the right key, and, in slow motion, it was inserted into the lock. Finally, slowly, loudly, it turned.

When Beethoven died and they performed an autopsy on his brain they found that there was not enough water in it. His brain was dried and shrivelled, bereft of the fluid of life. The doctors were puzzled. Did they not think that it might have been the Promethean fire that dried him out, that evaporated all the water away? The fire that burnt constantly within him, the artistic, creative fire, had finally burnt him out. It had been raging in his ears for many years until he had become deaf, and finally, after he had breathed so much life into his music, there was no longer enough to sustain himself.

If I think hard I can picture this fire, raging, coursing through his veins, emanating from his brain, the seat of his genius, the fountain of creation and beauty, the source of all his magic. Sometimes the flames can be seen leaping out of his nostrils, or steam shwooshing out of his ears as he works. His face is red with the heat, but still it burns inside him, uncontrollably, unquench-able.

They were not expecting to find me there, just as I was not expecting to see them. Their faces were red and traumatised, and I knew instantly that Bryony was dead. There were no clues to this other than the very fact that they were there, with their corporately concerned faces, their mouths opening but producing no words. They stood awkwardly, shifting their feet as they spoke, and I let their words fly in waves over my head. Some of them entered my ears, fewer still my brain. I hung my head, my jaw dropped almost to the floor, my eyes felt as though they would burst from the pressure of the tears that queued up behind the ducts and yet for some reason refused to escape as yet.

Bryony was a beautiful, sensual woman. I had been so often caressed by her musical words as they flowed from her mouth, transfixed by the way her hair flowed around her face, the smile that she threw out at me now and again that made me melt into her existence. The accomplished way she would put her hand to her head and scratch the top of it when she was puzzled about something. At such times, as always, the dura mater lurked beneath her skull, just out of reach of her fingers, a tough layer lining the inside of her skull.

Inside this dura mater nestled her arachnoid membrane, soft

and serous, thin, a smooth polished surface covering the inside of her dura mater. Then, inside that, the pia mater; blood vessels held together by areolar tissue. Three concentric spheres, membranes, separating the workings of her brain from the outside world.

In between her arachnoid and pia maters was her subarachnoid space. Narrow on the surface of the hemispheres, wider at the base of the brain, this cavern was filled with a clear, limpid fluid with a saltish taste – cerebrospinal fluid. At some time, I don't know when, she began to bleed into this subarachnoid space. As the blood vessels divided at the base of her skull, in a process known as bifurcation, a berry aneurysm developed. This enlarged, thinned, stretched, and eventually ruptured. This was a subarachnoid haemorrhage. For those last moments in her room that evening, and for some amount of time before that, blood was entering her subarachnoid space, and I didn't know it.

I don't know what any of this means. I didn't recognise any of these processes in her. How could I have known? Why wasn't I told about it so that I could warn her, prevent it from happening? How could I have been happily sipping the wine and eating the chocolate and letting the Beethoven swirl its shapes around me and not have known what was happening to her? They sawed through her skull in the post-mortem. Through the thick bone, the various membranes, and into the very centre of her head, where even I, who loved her, have not seen. I cannot imagine it. Her head, cracked open with a hammer and chisel, a saw run through it, the hair that I loved so much thick with her blood, somehow not yet clotted, not scabbed, but virulent red, full of the life that she no longer possessed. The membranes that were supposed to cover and protect her brain violated and open to assault.

No one has told me about the drama that must have been played out there on the staircase where she fell. I have never asked; but I have lived through it a million times inside my head. I can see her swirling elegantly down the stairs, her face full of smile, of the fun we were eating and drinking, of the wine she would return with. Then, she falls. She does not trip, or slide, she just falls, crumpled, inelegantly, undignified. At first people do not rush to help, thinking she has merely tumbled, but when she does not move they begin to react. I wonder at the bustle that must then have ensued. People are so reserved, so inside themselves. I suppose most of them pretended that nothing was happening, whilst keeping a close watch out of the corners of their eyes, satisfying their sick fascination for the macabre, the sick fascination that is in all of us. I can see them now, saying to each other, 'The poor girl, I hope she is all right,' while secretly they are thinking, I hope she dies – that would be a really dramatic thing to happen. People crave drama, excitement – anything to spice up their dreary lives, and the death of a fellow human being is something of the utmost fascination to all of us.

I wonder if she regained consciousness at all in between her fall and her death. I do not even know whether or not it was instantaneous. I know that she was pronounced dead the moment the useless medical people arrived. But how many agonising seconds, minutes, did she spend before she finally left this existence?

People sometimes tell stories of macabre and frightening things, and most of the details fly past us without being absorbed. Then suddenly a single detail, often one of the most innocent in the tale, strikes us, horrifies us, and we remember this element and the moment that we heard it for ever afterwards. I once knew someone who had been ill with a brain tumour, and had been coaxed to talk about it afterwards. I sat through the gory accounts of the medical instruments, the ins and outs of what had been done to his brain, the intimations as to how close he had come to being dead. Then, in the middle of a long and tedious account of his experience in the operating theatre and beyond, he mentioned in passing that the doctors had urged him, 'Whatever you do, don't fall asleep.' This was the central point of the story for me – the idea that there was some will, some human exertion involved. A weaker person may have simply given up all resistance and fallen into that everlasting sleep, but this man had fought, kept his eyes open, struggled with incessant and intense exhaustion, and had been rewarded with life. He did not say any of this. He did not need to. The image of all this fighting and suffering flashed over me at his simple words.

I wonder if there was anything for Bryony to fight. I wonder if Bryony would have survived had she fought it. I think my greatest fear is that she knew she was going to die. Television and films and novels and various other media give us differing accounts of the aspect of the dying person. I suppose there are as many different ways to die as there are people in the universe, but I can never believe that anyone is prepared to relinquish their life calmly and without resistance. I wonder if Bryony was awake inside even when she had already died for all intents and purposes. I wonder if she had lain there on the floor in pain, struggling to reach for her last chance at life, knowing that it was draining away from her but unable to express this ultimate emotion. The thought makes me shiver. Do I want to know the answer to this?

Did she feel any pain as she fell? Did she clasp her hands to her head in the hope that she could cradle away the agony? They told me that she would have lost consciousness almost instantaneously. What does this mean? Was there a moment when she knew? The headache would have begun at the base of her skull and spread quickly. She might have vomited; I don't know, no one has told me. I want to know if she suffered any awareness of her impending mortality. I want to get inside her head in those last moments and know what was happening there, not the haemorrhage and the blood and the suffocating brain cells, but the *mind* part of her head. I want to know if she saw her life in monochrome sequences in front of her eyes; if there was a white flash and *boom!* she was dead; if she had seen angels or had walked down a tunnel leading to a gate with dead friends and relatives on the other side.

I reach into my bag and pull out my copy of *Gray's Anatomy*. 'The cranial cavity contains the brain. Its boundaries are formed by the bones of the skull,' it shouts at me. That first day I had talked about shoulders. Bryony's shoulders were innocent and free of burden, still intact. Yet they had to die when her brain did. Had her shoulders been chipped off, her brain could have survived and she would still be alive. Her shoulders were exposed to the world, covered by only layers of thin material at most – vulnerable, accessible. Her brain was protected by many layers of different types – crisp ones, spongy ones, fluids and shock-absorbers – yet the attack came from within, and she had no defences against it.

In the rivers of her brain, there was an enemy. In the caverns that her head contained there was an unwelcome visitor, an adversary, stronger than she was, fluid and able to destroy. The enemy had been flowing through her veins, her heart, rivulets of life that sustained her and enabled her body to function. Red flames that she could not have lived without, but that nevertheless killed her. The little cells invaded the cave of her subarachnoid space, played like children in their new openness, into which they had squeezed themselves mischievously. The blood was part of her. The blood was her very life and her very death. What is it we live by if it is not death?

I wonder about my capacity for happiness. I have pulled myself out of the abyss of shock and depression I fell into during the days immediately following Bryony's death, and I know it is natural to still be grieving after such a short time. I am nevertheless not sure whether I shall ever be able to take a look at my life and say, 'I am happy.' Is happiness something that you can only experience in the extreme short term? Standing at the top of a hill and looking at the rows of houses and cars, the winding roads, expanses of water; that is happiness. Driving into a peach-coloured sunset; looking at a vivid sky through bright droplets of rain. These are the things that uplift my spirit. Most of the time I don't think about whether or not I am happy. I just get on with life and try not to question too much, as most of us do. If was to perform an experiment on myself, asking myself at random intervals, 'Am I happy?' I know that the 'no's would far outnumber the 'yes's.

For some reason I visited her in the chapel of rest before her body was removed in preparation for the funeral. I am not sure what possessed me. Perhaps I felt that I had been cruelly deprived of the last moments of her life and I wanted to regain by some miraculous trick what I thought I had lost. She should have died in my arms. I should have felt the last throbs of life drain out of her, she should have slumped with the force of death against me. The last beatings of her heart should have been mine, should not have happened alone against the sterile stair carpet of the hotel. The hands that touched her were those of strangers. I could give her nothing, nothing, in those last seconds of her life. I was remote, useless. I was alone in her room waiting for her return, not knowing that it would never come. I must have sat there in happiness for many minutes after she had died, knowing nothing of her expiry; cheerful, while she was lying motionless in death.

I tried to silence my footsteps – I do not know why, but it was certainly not for fear of waking her – as I walked across the soft-tiled floor to where her body lay. For a moment, just as I reached the spot where I would first have seen her over the sides of the coffin, I closed my eyes, not wanting to see. I felt that with a sufficient exertion of my will the coffin would be empty, or she would be sitting up in it confused and frightened but alive. When I finally opened my eyes, waves of shock ran through my body. She was still and peaceful, as though in a sleep – like the sleep she had been in that morning when I woke up with her – but her breast did not rise and fall as it should have done, and a strange coldness emanated from her. Her face was as white as the silk lining of the coffin, her cheeks almost hollow with whiteness, more pale than anything I had seen.

I wanted to cup those cheeks in my hands and redden them once more; I wanted to fuse my lips with those of the sleeping girl and breathe life back into her face which now wore a hue still paler than in life. Golden-brown hair was framing her face as always, death permitting her mouth to let escape that hint of a smile that she always wore. I wept with ferocity, breathing in the familiar essence of the girl, and slowly exhaled, scattered images filling my mind. Almost unconsciously, I drew the lifeless body towards me and buried my face in that still glorious hair. Bryony's skin was soft against my fingers, and there was some-thing of a freedom exuding from it, something that had been unable to escape in life. She was beautiful. Overcome with love, with loss, with a million emotions that I cannot begin to name, I put my mouth to her ear and whispered, 'I am yours,' creasing my face in an effort to stop the tears, but to no avail. I half-remembered a desire to caress this skin, a desire felt in times when I had not known such desolation. I kissed the dead girl's lips, secretly hoping for something of Juliet's sensation in the tomb, but instead was rewarded with a cold, sterile non-response. Bryony was dead. I was thrown into a final acknowledgement of this harsh fact.

That night I dreamed that her brain had been invaded by an army of spiders. Spiders, arachnids, murderers. They crept into her head and silently worked to bring about her death. I didn't know; I was keeping a watch on her, protecting her, responsible for her well-being, but I didn't see it happening. I didn't know until she fell to the floor dead, when the spiders poured out of every orifice in her head: her ears, her mouth, her nostrils, even from behind her eyes, and then they started emanating from her pores. When I awoke, the sweat was crawling over my body like spiders, and I had to shake myself again and again before I really believed that it had been a dream. Perhaps not only the spiders, but the whole reality of her death had been an imagining of my sleeping brain. Bryony might still be alive. I tried desperately to believe this but I knew that all was real. The tears started to fall, then to gush, mingling with the hot sweat on my face and neck, until I felt that I was swimming in a hot sea of disbelief.

Satisfaction is a difficult thing to come by. Immediate emotions can be satisfied, needs and desires can be fulfilled, but in the large arc of our lives we can never have everything that we want. We desire so much, so contradictingly, that we could never have everything were we to live for a million years. It is also because however much we have, we still want more. A tramp lying in the gutter would give anything he could for a squalid flat to live in. Give him such an abode and he will be overwhelmed with joy until he becomes accustomed to it – for a few hours, weeks, or months if he is so disposed – and then he will start yearning for something better. The lord in his mansion does not possess everything that he desires. There is always something just out of reach.

And what would happen if we were to have everything? Imagine, for a moment, that you have everything you could ever want. Your life is complete. What do you do when you get up in the morning? Perhaps you read books, now that you can afford as many as you like. Thus, you betray a thirst for knowledge, which would mean you do not yet have everything you desire after all, which is the prerequisite for the scenario. So begin again. You have everything and you know everything. Indeed, to make the concept still tighter, imagine that anything you desire you have in the instant that you desire it. How do you entertain yourself? There is no point in travelling because you see it all instantly. You cannot take up a new hobby, as simply the interest in it provides you with all the knowledge, all the equipment, all the ability to become an instant expert.

All you can do is keep yourself clean, feed yourself, keep your body alive and healthy. A bored hamster in a cage made up of possessions; trapped by acquisitions. Life is about strife and struggle. Perhaps we are not supposed to be happy. Perhaps there is no such thing as happiness, but it is an illusion conjured up by this whole sorry species as a way of using our intelligence, the mixed blessing that we have somehow evolved. There is only immediate emotion. Long-term coherence is simply fiction; we have invented it because we have memories and we can put every event of our lives into these memories and manipulate them to fit in with our view of ourselves.

I did not go to the funeral. I was not invited, simply because her family knew nothing of me. I am told it was a quiet affair: a few family members, a little speech about her achievements and qualities, and her memory was flung out into the world of the buried. If I had been there, I doubt I would have recognised *my* Bryony from the descriptions and tributes. I can picture the flowers, the scribbled messages hanging from their stalks by a limp piece of string. I expect it rained as her coffin was lowered into the ground; it always does. Or perhaps there was bright sunshine and blue sky, bright petals and leaves just turning into their autumn colours. There will have been tears from her mother, consoling looks from the group of mourners in their self-consciously black clothes and their slick hair. I am glad I didn't have to wave her off in that way.

I didn't know Bryony's family, her mother, her father, her sisters. I imagined her mother to look very much like an older version of her, perhaps with more exaggerated features. Formed as the lines and angles in her face had aged and toughened in preparation for the day when they would snap in their elderly brittleness. Her father I supposed to be strong, in both a physical and a mental sense, in the way that fathers are supposed to be strong. Of her sisters I knew nothing, other than that she had three. A houseful of little girls growing up together must have helped to form the Bryony she had become when I knew her.

It is difficult to think of Bryony surrounded at her funeral by these anonymous people. It is as though she had two lives; one for them and one for me. Perhaps she had further lives that I knew nothing of. No; she could not have concealed anything from me. I would not have recognised the Bryony that they sent off into the abyss of the buried because it was not the same Bryony that I knew. The only person at *my* Bryony's sending-off was me.

I took the day off, just as I had with Bryony on the last day of her life, but this time with the full understanding and approval of the company. I think I cried continuously for the whole day, but it is another area in which my memory is frustratingly yet comfortingly blank. I walked around the grounds of the hotel, I walked miles out into the countryside, I went to the sea, I walked and walked and walked until my feet hurt and my head ached with the constant pain of the sun and the wind in my eyes. Still the pain of my loss became greater each second. I remember standing on the sand by the edge of the water, squinting into the sun, my hair blowing in all directions around my face, every now and then a gritty piece of sand flying up at me.

I bent and picked up a sea-smoothed pebble, feeling its cool-ness in my hands for a few moments. It was a dappled grey in colour, almost a flat oval but with a little more three-dimension-alness about it. I ran my fingers over it and felt all the little lumps and bumps, felt its smoothness from the constant dashing of the sea. How can something as rough and violent as the constant barrage of waves produce something so smooth and rounded? The corners had not been chipped off but rather caressed away until they just were not there. I pressed it to my lips; it felt cold and stern, and alienly unfamiliar.

Then I tossed it nonchalantly into the water, held on to the sight of it with my eyes until the moment it broke the skin of the water and fell in. Slithers of waves were breaking around my feet, and some of my tears fell into them, mingling my own salt with the great mass of it swirling and sweeping from shore to shore with the ocean. Every now and then a wave appeared that was larger and stronger than its colleagues, and one startled me by soaking my shoes and reaching inland for a good distance. I stared down at my feet and responded to it with a sullen, 'You still don't scare me.' The next thing I remember is falling to my knees in the soggy sand oblivious to everything but my tears, my loss, the enormous void in my life.

Sand, covering my knees, my ankles, my feet, my hands, my wrists. Sand in my mouth, in my ears, gritting my eyes, coating my hair. It could have buried me in its perfect graininess. The sound of the ocean, free, alive and permanent, spiralling its journey down my auditory canal, through my middle ear and finally gushing into the labyrinth of my inner ear, seeping wildly into my brain where it swirled endlessly with strains of Beethoven and the grains of sand that seemed to have got in there too. I could pour water and sand into Bryony's ears, I could amplify them to a million times their proper volume and she still would not hear. The echoey chambers of her brain have filled themselves with blood and killed her with her own hot, warm fluid; there is no room for sound, or sights, or tactile sensations.

Sand, floating around in the air, even though there is no wind. Sand, everywhere I look, getting into everything the way it always does at the seaside. Yet it cannot penetrate Bryony now. It could cover the shell of her body but she could not feel its grains pressing into her soft skin. It could get into her eyes, her mouth, but she would not blink or spit. It could find a resistless home in Bryony's body, just as the worms and the spiders will do when the earth settles on her coffin. The spiders did not kill her but they will live in her. They will move in and out of the doors in her body, just as in my dream, and she will not be able to fight them.

I wanted to feel her comforting hands on my shoulders, to hear the perfect orchestra of her voice whispering words of consolation. But the rabid conductor had killed the players, destroyed their instruments, then shot himself in the heart. I could not even find the spot where we built our sandcastle because the sea had a million times changed the beachscape. Altered it, by sweeping up on to it and carrying its different parts into its own vast body, exchanging them for other parts which have perhaps been swimming for some time. I tried to place the spot by the cliff patterns, but even they were changing, though not as rapidly. There were no birds screeching in the perching caves today, no wind-blown gulls dashing over the water. They must have known. The beach was a different place.

When I was a child, the old woman from next door died suddenly one Christmas. My bed was arranged so that I slept with my head next to the window, and if I moved right up against the headboard I could see up into the gap between the window sill and the curtains out into the night. When I went to bed that night, I could feel Mrs Wilson's face, greatly enlarged, looking in at me through the window. I knew that if I looked I would find nothing there, yet I was terrified to find out just in case I was wrong.

My father came in to see me in the middle of the night, obviously aware that I was still awake and restless, and I confided my fears to him. He put his face close to mine, so close that I could smell the remnants of the cigarette he had smoked before bed, and said, 'You know that if she was out there she wouldn't hurt you.' He had meant to comfort me but his words flooded me with a greater fear; I had thought my ideas were just childish fancies, but his acknowledgement that they were possible swept away those attempts at consoling myself, and I felt the cold hand of the afterlife on my shoulder.

My grandmother died not long after, and in the nights following I had the same sensation, but this time I steeled myself to look, and discovered once and for all that her face was nowhere but in my imagination. I was greatly comforted, but now I wish that I had seen something, an apparition, a smiling, contented face. I want to feel that Bryony is still with me, somehow, that I have not lost her, that she is not unreachable. I was never her lover and yet I am mourning her as though I was. I miss the tangles of her hair against my face in the morning, the creases in her body from being pressed up against the wrinkled sheets all night long. I miss her clothes crumpled on my floor, her soft kisses on my cheek, our arms about each other's waists on long country walks. These things were never real, yet I miss them.

I was empty. There was nothing left now. No, it was more than that; not an absence, but a solid, dark presence. I wanted my life to drain out of me, to feel a limpness creeping over me, and finally to be enveloped by sweet darkness. Wherever I went I saw emptiness, hanging in shards, great grotesque shapes, the shapes of my grief, lurking, threatening.

I never felt suicidal during those days in Peterborough. Then it was merely that I wanted none of the things that I had, including my life, my existence. Now this was reversed. I wanted to actively disperse the ghosts that were pursuing me. My life was a monstrous tormentor and I wanted to relieve myself of it, to escape from the pain. Panic and emptiness. The panic, the emptiness, they were tangible, they pressed themselves against my face, they made my sheets cold and damp at night. Blasted with sighs, and surrounded with tears; there was no hiding place. I wanted to feel the release of death. I waited for it. I willed it to find me. But it never came.

*

By the front door there is a smell of forsythia and lavender. The combination produces a sickly odour that always reminds her of the perfume her mother keeps in a shiny bottle on her dressing table. The grass was well kept before the children grew to be able to run but now it is trampled and squashed, and no daisies grow any more. She likes to pick daisies. She knows how to make them into chains and wear them around her neck. This makes her feel like a princess.

The cat is not in the front garden. She looks to her brothers for confirmation of this, and they make large grins that go from one ear to the other. 'Freeeeezing cold.' She steps deliberately towards the passage entrance, and can tell by their staged gestures that this is correct. The sad little girl is once again in the passage. The walls are almost black, not from the colour of the bricks or from paint, but from many years of people breathing as they walked through. Her parents sometimes smoked cigarettes, and they smoked them here if it was raining; they never smoked inside the house because it made the children ill. Some of the mortar towards the ceiling was crumbling away, although she was never quite sure that the passage had a ceiling. The walls got more and more curvy as they went upwards, until they met in the middle, and if there was a ceiling, she did not know where the wall ended and it began. She supposed that adults had answers to such things, and she would know when she had finished growing up.

★

I suppose I have grown up now. I thought I had grown up when I waved goodbye to my mother from the window of my student room at eighteen, but I didn't know how much further I still had to go. Now I don't feel that I have grown up. I am still a child, alone now that Bryony, on whom I had rapidly become as dependent as a child upon a mother, has left me. I want to crawl into a bright Wendy house and cry the wild yet soon abated tears of a toddler. I do not want to have to cry adult tears; they hurt more and they are difficult to stop. I do not want to go back to my adult life where I have to pretend that everything is all right and I have not suffered this great loss. I want to proceed backwards into my own history.

Telephone

I suppose I should have said something to Joe about Bryony's death. I should have let him support me, as I know he would have wanted to. I should have told him about the things that were happening in my head and in my heart. Perhaps it was my lack of confidence in him that began to prise apart the cracks that were already forming in what I had thought was the infallible cement of our relationship. I am not really sure why I didn't tell him. I had mentioned her during our brief calls before the phone in our new house had finally been connected, but I had been very careful to avoid telling him how much she meant to me. Perhaps I was fearful of his becoming jealous, or perhaps I was ashamed of myself for feeling so close to someone else when I was about to embark on my life with Joe. There is another possibility though: I think I was so very confused about my feelings, many of which I had not been able to acknowledge even to myself, that there really would not have been anything to tell him.

At the time of her death I was just beginning to put names to some of the emotions I was suffering. Perhaps the word 'suffering' is not a good one, because I was happily enduring them for the most part. Yet at the same time they were causing me a great deal of anguish. Although I had formed no solid images in my mind, every now and then I experienced – not imagined, or visualised, or thought, because its form was nothing as definite as any of those – a wave of anticipation of life with Bryony. Somewhere in the back of my mind were pictures of an ultimate partnership formed with Bryony, a partnership continued and spent throughout in ecstasy. She made my future look like a warm glow.

I knew that being with Joe would be good, that I would enjoy it, that it would be good for me. I knew that I would find a comfortable niche in his arms, in which I could rest and be a real, solid member of the world. I knew that I had once felt an amber delight at the thought of seeing him for the weekend, that I had once had that knot in my stomach when he put his hands on me or kissed me. But Bryony took hold of that practical knot and pulled it into many new and unfamiliar shapes, forming new knots that I had never heard of and that didn't seem to fulfil any useful function but that I nevertheless coveted. Some people fill their houses with neat, practicable furniture where they can hide the ugly items of necessity, comfortable sofas, curtains that pull with the greatest ease. Others prefer the bulky ornamentation of antiques.

The rafters of King's Cross are vast, and support large expanses of roof that stop the sky from flooding the station. On what kind of adventure am I setting out from here? I feel that the adventure is already over but I am reminded that I do not know. Penzance, Bryony, the beach, the seagulls, the hotel; it could all be an insignificant prelude to some still larger episode. I feel the blood in my veins turn a little colder at the idea. I thought I was going home: but am I?

I am reminded of Forster's idea that the stations of London or indeed of any venue take on the character of the places to which they are the gateways. Sitting here at King's Cross I feel infinitely closer to Durham than I did at Paddington, although I have travelled but a short part of the distance. The whole building seems to cry out at me 'The North! Peterborough! Durham!'. And then there is beyond, to Scotland, to the lochs and the mountains, the heather and the thistles, but these are not part of my journey.

At last the train begins to pull off, and the grinding clattering of the stationary engine gives way to the slightly smoother gliding sound of motion. The huge, airy and yet airless shed of King's Cross starts to recede and the evening sunshine makes its way in through the windows. My companions squint at the sudden invasion of sunbeams, but I welcome them. It was cold and dark in the station, and it always delights me to emerge from it into the real day, as though I cannot believe that the sun is still there if I am unable to see its light or feel its warmth.

When Bryony died, I suppose some part of my brain decided that the best thing to do would be to pretend, on the surface, that she had never existed. I could live out all my silent torment inside my own self, and give nothing of this away to other eyes, Joe's in particular. The knowledge of my terrible loss, I thought, might harm our relationship, might drive me further from him than I had already come.

It was only a few days after the funeral, and thus after I had attempted to say goodbye to her by means of some kind of proxy funeral inside my head, that Joe's – our – telephone was connected to the outside world. We were suddenly able to communicate properly, at least in a physical sense. I dialled his number from the matt white phone beside my bed, almost shaking with the resolve to keep the whole matter secret from him.

'Hello?' came the familiar and yet by now less routine voice of my lover.

'Hi, Joe!' I beamed down the line at him.

'Angel! How are you?'

I always found this obligatory exchange of pleasantries at the start of a call embarrassing, and I did my best to sweep them away as rapidly as possible. 'Fine, thanks. You okay?'

'Yes, I suppose so. I'll be much better when you get home, though.'

A tinge of guilt passed through my shoulders, up into my neck and spiralled upwards, finally reaching my head and making me dizzy. I tried to work out why I felt so guilty but I did not let myself search too hard.

There was a short, stiff silence as we again tried to think of what we could say to each other. I suppose Joe's difficulty was that he had so many things he wanted to say to me, that were threatening to pour out all at once, that he had to try to put them into some kind of order before he could say anything at all. Mine was rather different. I realised suddenly how difficult saying nothing about Bryony would be. The last week of my life had been spent completely immersed in tragedy, in loss, in Bryony, and I had thought and done little else. Yes, I had dragged myself into sessions each day and tried my utmost to give the appearance that I was paying attention, to put a sunny veil over my face that would hide the dark, lethargic clouds that still hung over me, but my mind had been elsewhere.

'How are you getting on then? Learnt anything exciting?'

'Oh, yes,' I lied. I immediately realised that he would recognise this to be an untruth, and I tried to pretend that the remark had been intended as a sarcastic one. 'I know all kinds of exciting things now.' I wished I could have thought of something more witty to say, but I was struggling. I wanted to cry, I wanted to throw the receiver on to the floor and cry out huge, heavy tears that would drag themselves slowly down my face and make huge blobs when they reached the carpet. It was difficult to say nothing about the events of the previous week for a different reason than the one I had anticipated – for suddenly I almost wanted to. My admirable plans of dishonesty and deception had failed me and I wanted to pour it out over him, now my only confidant. The words were stuck at the back of my throat, as if with a piece of infinitely powerful Blu-tak, which had the dual purpose of both sticking them there and forming an obstruction in my throat, due to which I had to work extra hard to be able to speak or indeed breathe.

'Anyway, the phone's all working now, as you can see. It's so nice to have a phone again – I hardly realised how much I missed it! Not as much as I miss you, though.'

I winced at his soppiness, even though he had been careful to tinge it with an edge of humour. 'I miss you too,' I crooned back at him. I wasn't lying. Suddenly I wished I was at home with him and that I could enfold myself in his arms and weep the tears that lay behind my eyes until I was satisfied that no more would follow. I would tell him about Bryony, I knew that, but I did not want to tell him over the telephone. It was too important; and besides, I knew I would cry, and I wanted to spare us both the frustration of the unfulfilled need to comfort and be comforted.

I take out my portable CD player, feeling the need to listen to some music. Opening up the case, I find that the Beethoven is still inside. I begin to remove it, sadly, but then I change my mind. I run my thumb around the edge of the CD, hearing the boisterous tones of the symphony inside my head, and finally reach for the headphones. Schopenhauer felt that Beethoven's symphonies inspired a plethora of feelings and emotions that overwhelmed the listener at one and the same time, 'like a world of spirits without material'. Perhaps listening to the Seventh Symphony again will return Bryony to me. She is without material, without a physical body, but her spirit is still intense in my veins. It has often been said that Beethoven was a sort of Prometheus, magically casting men from tone rather than clay; will he cast Bryony for me now, from the silver shining of the CD and the metal and plastic of my player? If I let myself live through my ears, just for a moment, will she exist again, be real again, not just in my mind, but in the tangible reality of the music?

Then he shot the bolt at me. 'How's Bryony getting on? Is she finding it as tough as you are?' I expect my silence didn't last as long as I felt it to but there must have been a noticeable pause. I took a large, deep breath, as noiselessly as I could, trying to fill my lungs with any strength that might be in the air around me, but most of that air stuck against the Blu-tak in my gullet, and I achieved nothing.

'She's fine.'

'Good.' A long pause, and then, 'Good.'

'The house is still okay, then?' I put in quickly. 'You haven't wrecked it yet?'

'Hmph. What are you expecting me to do?'

'I wish I could see it.' This was genuine. Now that Bryony was no longer there, part of me couldn't wait to get away from Penzance, as far away as possible, back to something familiar, to something that held no memories of her. I was sure that I would find reminders everywhere I looked, wherever I looked, for some time to come, but I wanted to be away from the place where I had done so much with her, felt so much with her. 'It's so frustrating being here and knowing that you have had free reign with everything.'

This was more comfortable territory, yet I still found myself uneasy, and spoke with difficulty. I wondered why Joe had not noticed. Perhaps he had and was putting it down to the length of our separation, or the intensity and exhaustion of the course. Still, I waited for him to ask me what was wrong, not knowing what I would say when the question finally came.

Did she clutch her head with pain, the dreadful, unstoppable pain that began at the base of her head and spread like a flame around it? Her hands moving over the soft hair that coated her skull, the pain rancid beneath them? Did her eyes, so recently blotched and stained from wretched crying, screw themselves tightly up in an effort to bear or banish the agony? Did she feel the pain without knowing the pain? Was it so fierce that it blotted out her mental faculties? Did she stand thus for a moment, or longer, in ugly, clenched pain, before her beautiful, tormented body dropped like a leaf from a tree to the floor? Did she stumble, winded by the pain, and attempt to get help before the final, blinding blow hit her? Her arms outstretched towards strangers begging them for help, her mouth wordless from the pain?

Finsbury Park denotes the outer reaches of the capital. It is one of those areas that still feels like London when one is on foot, yet does not from the confines of the train. I want to look at the one photograph I have of Bryony, and I pull the brightly coloured sleeve of pictures out of my bag. There she is, at the front of the pack, the corners of the paper worn with use. She is smiling, as she always is, or always was. Her hair is neatly tucked behind her shoulders, but I can see the very ends peeking out by the side of her arm. The sandcastle that she built – that we built – has been swept away now, just as she has, and there is only an empty spot where both sat.

I pull out the other picture – the one of me beside our castle – and, with shaking fingers, I put them together just the way Bryony did. I have not allowed myself to attempt this since her death, but I need to see that picture of happiness. I need to feel that there is still some connection between us. The two decorated lumps of sand slowly melt into one another as I slide one piece of paper across the other, until the moment when their shapes and lines meet, and there is a picture of us, the three of us, all smiling in the sunshine. One never alive, one once alive and now dead, and me, the sole survivor.

'I keep looking at that calendar you gave me, you know. I've marked the date with a big yellow sticker – I couldn't bear to deface it!'

'Aah!' I crooned.

'At least it's on the right page now. It seemed so far away when I had to keep peeking over the page to see it, but now it's there for everyone to see, even if it is right at the end of the month.'

'God, I'm not looking forward to the journey home. It seemed like for ever getting here, and it's going to be even worse when I'm actually coming home to you. I can't believe I have to change so many times.'

'That's London for you – in the middle of the country and in the way of everything.'

'Hey!' I always felt a little defensive of my home town, even though I did not like it all that much myself. It seemed a personal insult when people were derogatory about it, and I could never resist leaping in. I heard him grin at the other end of the line, and decided to say nothing more on the subject.

There are tears falling out of my eyes, but still I stare at the picture. I am careful not to let the wet drops drip on to the only image of Bryony that I have outside my mind. I let them fall down my cheeks and on to my lap; little moist blobs that will soon deteriorate and disappear just as our sandcastle did. I wish that we could have built something more permanent, something that I could carry with me in a suitcase through my life, something that I could hold in my hands knowing that Bryony had helped to create it.

★

Little red-shoed feet tiptoe down the narrow strip of land between the long shed and Mrs Wilson's fence. The sweet peas peep down at her over the wide part of the fence at the top, and push their tendrils softly through the gaps between the slats, offering her their leafy encouragement. Mrs Wilson is a kind old woman with hair that is white and balances thinly on the top of her head. The little girl can hear her in the garden on the other side of the fence, and holds her breath for fear that she might provoke curiosity in her neighbour. Her tiny steps take her slowly along the bed of soggy earth, and her shoes pick up the cakes of mud and stop being so red. Cries of 'Warmer! Warmer!' lead her on, and she continues, yet she wonders where there is a hiding place for a cat in this dingy cut.

At last, she reaches the raggedly piece of fence that separates her from the adult part of the garden, and stops. There is an entrance to this area but the gate is kept locked, and the children are not allowed to enter without their parents. Marcus and Daniel must have been misleading her, so she turns back and retraces her steps. They laugh and tell her she is becoming colder. As she walks, the temperature continues to drop and she actually begins to shiver, perhaps with the imagined cold, or maybe it is the despair and frustration that she is feeling. They must have been lying to her; the cat is not in this place. She tries one last time, and heads again for the makeshift fence, wondering if she has missed something, but again, finds nothing. Her thoughts are by now twisted with confusion, and she spins back and forth, in a circle, to the excited, mocking cries of 'Warmer! Colder! Warmer! Colder!', her tears starting to spill over the churned up ground.

*

I have told Joe little about my childhood; I have never said much about it to anyone. It is not that my memories are particularly bad ones; rather that they are very personal and I don't think other people would find them of any interest. I have sat through the reels and reels of other people's pasts too many times to risk making that much of a fool of myself. In any case, there are so many blanks in what I can remember of my life in London that I would never be able to make a coherent story out of it in the way that other people seem to. I am sure they employ a bit of creative gap-filling. It seems impossible that anyone can hold details from every part of their lives in their heads. When we dream, it is said, we dream of garbled images, isolated events that bear little or no relation to one another. It is only after we wake that our brain, unaided by our consciousness, makes them into a story, or usually several stories, that we can relate to ourselves and to other people.

Life frequently seems like that to me. The structure that we impose upon it is simply an artificial skin. If we peeled it off like that of a banana, we would reveal a jumbled mess of parts with no skeleton to hold them together. Perhaps we could then pick them up and arrange them as we chose, to create a better end result, if only we were able to get under the skin. Alas, it is too well moulded, too durable, too fierce, and too necessary. Those who achieve such a feat, who realise that their whole life previously has been nothing but a collection of isolated events, are put into madhouses and forced to live outside the comfortable, imagined cohesion of society.

A symphony is traditionally made up of four movements. The four movements are in some way related, whether it be by key, by themes – perhaps a theme from the first movement returns in the last, often somehow altered – or by some other commodity. A movement alone is made up of a number of sections. The first movement of a Classical symphony is usually in the form of a sonata. The sonata is made up of two sections, either of which may or may not be repeated. The first section has one main period, while the second has two. Each period is made up of a number of subsections, which are in turn comprised of themes, which are in turn comprised of phrases, which can be broken down infinitely into subphrases, the smallest component being, of course, the individual note. Many levels of structure are at work simultaneously, and all combine to form a coherent musical work.

In Classical science, the atom was thought to be the smallest element of matter, and parallels can thus be drawn between it and the musical note. Modern physics has shown us that there are indeed many smaller levels, and quantum physics has thrown the whole area into confusion, but we can let this pass, just in the same way we can forget for now that a musical tone is made up of smaller, equally subdivideable components.

Atoms, like the tiniest events in a person's life, and like the individual notes of a symphony, combine to form things that combine to form things that combine to form things which in turn combine to form still higher things. The process continues ad infinitum. Even something which we may think is complete – say a person – is part of a larger system (the Earth) containing air and water and other people and insects. The Earth is part of a solar system, which in turn belongs to a galaxy, a universe… and then what? We don't know. In music, a complete work may not be the end of it. A Wagner opera may be combined with others to form a cycle. A number of cycles may be combined with other works to form a composer's opus. A number of composers may be together classified as a style or era.

Physical existence does a pretty good job of coherence; it must do, because without it none of us would exist, and besides, it has the infallible (and as yet unknown to man) rules of nature to assist it. Music is an art, and as such, a certain structure and development is implicit in it. But history is different. History is something that can be interpreted in different ways by different people and collapses ultimately into a blob, a pool of events. We try to impose structure on it because it helps us to predict the future and because it helps to confirm our image of the world and ourselves as something meaningful, and therefore real and significant. But the more real we try to make things, the more artificial they actually become.

'It sounds like it's not as bad as you thought it was going to be, at least,' said Joe, after I had given him a summary of some of the activities I had taken some notice of. I felt guilty for lying to him – and at this stage there could be no denying that I had lied – but I consoled myself with the promise that I would tell him the truth when I got home. I was surprised he hadn't been able to pick up on it yet. The more real we try to make things, the more artificial they actually become – and I had tried to be so genuine about my high spirits that they could not possibly have been real. Yet I detected nothing in his speech that hinted at any uneasiness, despite my close scrutiny of his words for such a sign.

'Yes, I suppose these things never are. I suppose nothing is ever as it seems.' I immediately regretted this attempt at wisdom. It was as though I was pushing him, daring him to notice a change in me, but he was still blind to it.

'Remind me... it will be about nine o'clock when you get home next Friday, won't it?'

'Yes.'

'Okay. Well, how do you feel about a celebratory meal?'

'Oh, Joe, I don't know... I'll be very tired. I don't know if I could face sitting in a restaurant after sitting in trains for all those hours.'

'No, no, I'll cook something for you.'

I laughed. 'You? Cook? Don't tell me you've been trying to better yourself in my absence?' He answered in the affirmative, and I was suddenly hit with a flash of what a good man he was. Of course I wanted to be with him. Just for a moment I had no idea what any of the doubts had been about, and a thread of that burning silk went through me, stirring something in me that had been still for the past week and that I had not felt for Joe in a much greater interval.

Hitchin. Arlsey. The train moves on, wheels ever turning, ever forward, the sleepers on the track pass, the minutes pass, the pages in the book of my story turn.

'Okay, that sounds wonderful. It will be nice to have a decent home-cooked meal, although having said that, the food here isn't that bad.'

'I should hope not, the prices they charge at that hotel,' he replied, as if chastising, despite the fact that I wasn't paying for any of it. Then he changed his tack and said, 'It's all right for some.'

I changed the subject. 'How's work, then?'

'Oh, pretty much the same as ever, really. Boring but they're still paying me, so I don't care.'

I had often reprimanded him for this attitude to his career, but really, I quite envied it. His level of stress was very low and he was able to blank himself off from the world during his working hours and simply get on with it. Certainly now I was jealous of that skill. I wished I could get Bryony out of my head; not forget her but have some control over my mourning so that I could banish this aching knot from my stomach. It might even have been the same one that she had tied there during her life, but, with her, it had died, and was starting to rot and stagnate inside me, falling into many pieces that floated about me, paining me in every part of my body.

I *had* to love Joe. Selfish though this sounds, I suddenly realised that he could put his own strong ropes in my body, cleanse me of Bryony's. With the knowledge of his love, and mine for him, I could be a real person again, I could stop living in the shadow of Bryony's death. I would go home to him, I would think of this in a glow of anticipation and I would make myself alive again, however much effort this required. I owed this much to myself, to Joe, and, in a peculiar sort of way, to Bryony.

The train has rattled through Biggleswade, and I look out at the Sandy countryside. The track here passes within a short distance of the RSPB reserve, and I can see the trees balancing at the top of the little quarry. The reserve is home to all sorts of creatures: squirrels, rabbits, deer, and of course, birds. How wonderful to be a bird, to spread one's wings and soar out from the branches of trees, high above all that is dull and dreary and monotonous – the sky one's oyster. I think of the little goldfinches that merrily peck at the string tying my parents' clematis to the trellis at nesting time; the blackbirds that hop around the garden floor tugging at worms, bursting into flight and their *chuck-chuck* alarm call at the appearance of any cats. In the distance, I can see the television transmitter that the birds must crowd on the top of, safe from human dangers and from any of the menaces that they encounter in the trees.

Was there pain elsewhere in her body? Did she feel her heart stop, the beating of her life wrench to a halt? Did ribbons of pain shoot across her chest as her arteries screeched out in gradual suffocation? Did her legs buckle under her in the distress that broke her body, her mind fighting to keep her up while her organs succumbed to that final need for sleep? Sleep? Did the pain reach to the tips of her fingers as she lay on the floor in her last moments, and finally flow out through them, a current, leaving in its wake only stillness, peace and death?

The sprawling Bedfordshire countryside very gradually becomes the stretch of The Fens. The early railway builders had trouble constructing a track over this boggy, marshy ground. The Fens is the only place I can go and not feel overcrowded. The towns and cities and even most of the countryside are full of swarming masses of people with their pushchairs and screaming children and their cars and radios, their lethal umbrellas and motorised wheelchairs. Stand at the top of a hill and there might be space all around you, but looking down you can see the sprawl of houses filling every available gap, and the snaky roads, the factories, the railways, the brown-grey mess of civilisation. Go to the bottom of a mountain and you feel dwarfed and trapped by it.

But in The Fens, you can take a bicycle and go along a flat, straight road until you are in the middle of a huge, flat expanse. Then you can look in any direction and all you can see is space – flat, clear, undeceptive space. There might be a row of watercolour trees on the horizon, or a line of cars motoring by in the distance, but there is never so much oppressive life – for other people's lives invariably are oppressive upon our own – that it squeezes your own life out of you in the same way that the air is squeezed out from the chimney when a house is full to the brim with people. Even in a rainstorm there is space. You can see through the rain, see it falling many miles away as well as close to your eyes. You can see the huge downpour of water from the sky and the area it covers and be reminded of how much water there is in the world, how much sky there is in the world, and that it is not completely full of ugly buildings and ugly people just yet.

'I hope you're not spending too much money on your holiday, anyway,' he joked.

I erupted at him, playfully, but was more offended than he could know by his frivolity. Bryony was dead: this was not a holiday. 'No, not really. We don't get any time to go out and spend money, and food and everything is all paid for, so I think I'm probably making a profit here.'

'What? No shopping?'

'Not really, no,' I said bluntly.

'I can't believe that Bryony hasn't taken you out on a spree. I know what you women are like when you get together.'

I sighed. I was restless, riled by the conversation. I suddenly didn't want to talk to him any more, didn't want to have to deal with the effort of concealing everything. I wanted to put the phone safely down and cover myself from head to foot with the duvet, bury myself, be oblivious to the minefield I was walking through. 'Talking of money, I suppose I ought to go. This will be costing me a fortune.'

'*Us*, dear,' he crooned. 'Costing *us* a fortune. What's yours is mine now and that includes the phone bill. Oh, and the other way round, of course.'

'Oh, thanks.' I couldn't resist a smile. His humour is that of a little boy at times, and yet I like it. It makes me feel comfortable. I know what is going on, where the joke lies, why it is funny, and I don't have to twist my brain in an effort to extricate the elaborate subtleties rife in some humour.

Soon, the openness gives way to the tangle of Holme Wood, where the younger trees dance mysteriously in the wind and the older ones bow sedately to one another as ancient trees are accustomed to do. There is not a great deal of Holme Wood left now. The trees have all been cut down and forced to comply with the selfish plans of man; a chair here, a wardrobe there, and a wood is no longer a wood. We are soon into Yaxley Cutting. Yaxley is an odd village. I took myself there on one of those dark days in one of my futile attempts to get the anvil of depression out of my chest. It is a long snake of a village that sits on a grey road, and the houses and shops are likewise grey and spiritless. The shopping centre is reminiscent of an inner-city slum, even though the countryside is so close and so light and airy. I think it is very much a dead village; the shops are closed, the petrol stations advertise their wares on cardboard signs, and most of the houses have tall, neglected grasses in their front gardens.

'I'll see you soon, anyway. There isn't long to go now.'

'It still seems like for ever, though.'

'Oh, come on,' I teased him, 'you're a big tough man. You can cope!'

'I love you, Angel,' he said, somewhat awkwardly despite having said it many times in the past.

I wanted to kiss him. It is difficult to say those words effectively, however truthful they might be, because of the huge weight of usage they have accumulated, but Joe used them beautifully, and I knew how much he meant them.

'I love you too.' The truth. There was a pause before our goodbyes – his reluctant, mine purporting to be. I was relieved to be alone again, even though this meant being prey to the wild thoughts that kicked and punched my head continuously. They had not gone away throughout our conversation, and I wanted to give way to them, to stop fighting them, to let my head fall on to my pillow and my mind and body into sleep.

The train is slowing down for its crawl into Peterborough. I pass the grimy site of Railworld, one of the dirtiest tourist attractions I have ever seen. The car park is a pile of concrete strewn with dents and loose gravel and potholes that become large untidy puddles at the slightest hint of rain. 'VISIT RAILWORLD' is painted in makeshift letters on a mock train sitting on a mock monorail, and behind it sit the Portakabins that serve as visitor centres. It was supposed to be a tourist attraction, to which rail enthusiasts would flock from across the country. Undeveloped though it may be, it is a reference point, a destination, a defining point of many journeys. Rail World – a world of journeys.

The path that slopes down to the river is a muddy track in the grass, carved out by the constant tramping of feet. The river itself is brown and murky and swoops untidily under the ugly iron railway bridge; a crossing point where two journeys might overlap, where two ships as it were (one being a train) might pass in the night. The river might be the scene of an entirely different journey, but all journeys are much the same. They have a starting point and an ending point and they pass through a number of different places, many of which are only seen for a second in passing, but all of which play a part in defining the journey as a whole.

Train tracks. Always the same distance apart. Rusted metal and cracked timber. Gravel and other stones and grass and brave, tough wild flowers. The tracks are always there, ever present, ever still. They don't look like a journey. You can walk on them at level crossings and at other places too if you climb through holes in wire fences or jump off station platforms. They are hard and solid, the stuff of reality, and they do not begin to imply that they can be the basis for a journey.

And then comes the train. It dances snakily along the track, to its own steely music. It whorls up passengers into its giant hollow body and they wend their way on its journey. Sometimes they go with it from start to finish, sometimes they join late or leave early. When the train approaches the platform, the station is filled with the jolly blasts of its wind, the metallic noise of its machinery, and all the people are filled with the smoke and spirit of the journey.

Beside Railworld is the arching town bridge, and the car park, where I once went to a funfair, alone and with the silver drops of tears making shiny rivulets from my eyes down to my chin. From there they spilled suicidally on to my neck, smashing into a million warm, damp specks. The city centre looms ever closer, although the train never enters it but skirts it sorrily, the track lying alongside the dregs of old railway lines and occasionally a fast food outlet or a DIY superstore. What images of Peterborough must be left with travellers who merely pass through, as indeed most of them (sensibly) do?

Did she hear a chorus of angels singing her to her death as she was torn out of life? Did she see a bright flash of pure white light and walk down a tunnel? Did she see every scene of her life played out to her on a long reel of film in the time that it took for her body to fall to the ground? She must have become an angel, if there are such things. She must be the most angelically beautiful one in all the flocks of them that sit above the clouds. She must swoop more gracefully, land with a touch of her toes on the ground more lightly, sing more sweetly than any other angel ever could.

Coordinates

Railworld passes in the blink of an eye. The grey-brown buildings of Finchley Green go by, along with office buildings, roads and roundabouts on the other side of the track. Under Crescent Bridge, resplendent in its blue and red coating, a stunning view of the District Hospital in its full glory, and finally, the station.

*

The child crouches by the small piece of fence at the end of the corridor. The wood is damper at the bottom, and the colour verges on green rather than the cleaner brown that is found higher up. Worms and snails have made their homes here, along with innumerable tiny creatures that she is unable to identify. At the very bottom there is a narrow gap, one that must have been at least enlarged recently, as the underside is drier and cleaner, as though it has not long been on the exterior. The tired girl lets her knees fall to the ground, and her dress becomes the same sticky brown as her shoes. She will be in trouble but she no longer cares. Her brothers have driven her this far and she intends to find her cat. They tell her that she is warmer now and she knows that they mean her to wriggle herself somehow underneath this fence. She fears the slimy mud that will cover her and the insects that will crawl close to her face. She fears also her mother's wrath, but she fears still more the plight of her cat, so she pulls herself tightly under the fence, through the gap, which will only just take her. Marcus and Daniel are laughing uncontrollably, but so heightened and intense is her mental state now that she hardly hears them.

The ground here is grey and white in places with ashes, and pieces of twig charred black crackle defeatedly beneath her feet. She has been to this part of the garden when the heap of black, white and grey has been engulfed in flames. She likes to see her father's bonfires. She likes the heat and the orange and the snowstorms of ash that coat the area around. Her mother never lets her get near but she does not mind, as she would be afraid of the fire if it was too close to her. She can see no hiding place for a cat here.

Marcus and Daniel have not followed her under the fence, but are clean and shiny and poking their heads over the gate, shouting, 'Hot! Boiling!' and shrieking with laughter. She moves closer to the bonfire, and realises that it is still smouldering enough to burn her if she is careless, and she backs away.

★

Peterborough. The final destination of a one-time journey, the unpremeditated stopping point of my travels and starting point of a life that was different from anything I had ever anticipated. That particular journey had begun in Manchester one rainy morning, although the small journey was only the final part of a much larger one, which I had unwittingly bought my ticket for long since. My passage away from Alan and Justin.

This passage took me to the railway station and on to a random train. I still don't quite know how I managed to disappear so effectively, or how I managed to stick to my resolve, but somehow it worked. After that soggy Monday morning, I never saw Alan or Justin again. It was all very cool and preconceived; I suppose that was the only way I could carry it out. That morning, as another week started, I think Justin knew that something was wrong, but I don't think he had an inkling as to the extent of my plans. I surprised myself with the amount of strength I possessed when I needed to draw on it. There was no way that he could have known what boiling waters lurked beneath the calm, liquid surfaces of my eyes.

He kissed me as he left for work. I was sitting at the long wooden table with my notes spread out around me, in the hope that I could create the impression of normality. I must have been at least partially successful, as he did not ask any searching questions. The last I saw of him was the bored look on his face as he glanced around the room and then back at me. He shut the door behind him. I heard the familiar sound of his engine starting, and through the net curtains I saw him drive away from me for the last time. I wondered idly if he would have stayed this time had he known, if he would have put me before his work just this once and tried to sort things out. Then I got up and wandered aimlessly into the kitchen and picked up a wooden spoon that was lying on the worktop; for some reason, one of my strongest memories of that day, despite everything, all the drama, all the uncertainty, is of gazing into the hollow, dead surface of that spoon. Unreflective, without the mirror qualities of its stainless steel cousins, who were all neatly hidden in the drawer. Taking the spoon with me, I picked up the phone and dialled Alan's number.

It was seven thirty in the morning, and Alan was asleep. I waited while the phone rang about a dozen times, until at last there was the crack of the receiver being lifted, and then a very tousled, 'Hello?'

'Hi, Alan, it's me.' I realised I was faking a smile, and reminded myself that I had only my voice with which to convince him.

'Angel, my Angel, What's wrong?'

It struck me how stupid, how obvious this plan was then, for the first time. I tried to calm my racing heart, and, my voice as deadpan as I could muster, answered with, 'Nothing. I just want to see you. I... miss you.' How phoney. But he swallowed it. I asked him to meet me at our regular rendezvous in the bowels of the city, and he said he would be there in an hour. I spent the next hour dashing through the house, shoving everything that was important to me into suitcases and rucksacks and then, when I ran out of sensible luggage, carrier bags. Now, as I stare at the plastic luggage beside me, I smile to myself at the difference. It was harder than I had imagined. I thought I did not possess much, but however much I shovelled into bags of some kind or another, the number of things I needed to take scattered around me still outside them seemed to remain constant. At eight twenty I slipped out of the flat and, with an umbrella as my only weapon against the sheeting rain, made my way gloomily through the sodden streets.

Peterborough was known long ago as Medehamstede, and later Burgh, because the wall built around the Saxon settlement made it resemble a city. Its skyline is dominated by the cathedral, which has had a chequered history. Building of St Peter's monastery began in 546 and finished in 633. It was burnt by the

Danes, and rebuilt a hundred years later, and in subsequent conflicts it was reputedly used for the stabling of horses. Many visitors agree that it is the city's only redeeming feature. In 1789 Byng asserted: 'Nothing can be worse built than Peterborough, or more melancholy,' and that, 'Peterborough is a mean built poor town.' Samuel Sidney wrote a hundred or so years later: 'Peterborough is one of the centres from which radiate three lines to London... there is therefore the best of all consolation in being landed in this dull, inhospitable city, that it is the easiest possible thing to leave it.'

I did not find it easy to leave Peterborough. Nor did I find it easy to live there, although I don't think that was Peterborough's fault. Staring out of the window at the station, now that we have stopped, I wonder how different it was one or two hundred years ago from today. Very different, I am sure; the development corporation that moved in here during the 1960s will have seen to that if no one else already had. I wonder, too, how much it has changed since my brief period of residency here. The city has so many associations for me that I am not sure how accurately I remember it. Perhaps I shall return one day and find out whether or not it really does possess the miserable and evil spirit I have in my mind endowed it with.

I was a little late, and I spotted Alan before he saw me. In the past I might have crept up on him and dug him in the ribs, but today was too important for cheap tricks. I stopped and stood on the spot, a few yards away from where he was standing, and waited for him to turn his head. In a few seconds he did and walked over to me. He kissed me, and I responded passionately, genuinely, fighting back the tears. I knew I would miss him, and realised how much I had underestimated this fact, overestimated my ability to switch off my feelings for him.

We dived into the Café Lotus, as usual, as quickly as we could in order to remain unseen. The thrill was gone for me. It no longer mattered whether or not we were discovered. Should a friend of Justin's be in town and notice us and get straight on his mobile phone, it would make no difference to anything – it was too late. It was already over. Now that the plan was formed in my mind, it seemed as though I had already put it into practice. As we

127

sipped the thick black coffee, I hardly noticed Alan for the dire thoughts that I was unable to dismiss from my melancholy mind. I let my eyes feast one last time on the beautiful shapes in his face, the open expression which told me repeatedly, without the need for words, that he loved me. My eyes ran like caressing hands over his chest, through his grey T-shirt and down to his waist, which, although I could not see for the table, my hands knew the feel of in great detail. I closed my eyes and pictured him removing his trousers, recapturing, just for a moment, that throbbing, liquid sensation between my legs; and then I was back in the real world, and again could not muster any enthusiasm for such concepts. I thought, I love you so much, Alan, and led him out of there, away from the sweet, meaty smell of fresh coffee and into the narrow streets.

I turned to face him, placed my arms tightly around his waist, and plunged my tongue into his mouth. The kiss was sweet, even heavenly, and just for an instant I thought I could not do it. My ideas of romantically running off into the night alone gave way to images of me and Alan, me and Alan, somewhere pretty, somewhere, anywhere, just together. I felt the tears pop like bubbles out of my eyes, and so did Alan. He kissed every little atom of flesh around them, and asked me the reason for my tears.

'I have to go,' I said. 'I'm going to miss you.' This was the truth.

He gave a love-ridden laugh. 'I'll miss you too, my Angel. I miss you every day.'

There was so much I wanted to say to him, so much that I continued wanting to say to him for a long time afterwards, but I held my tongue and walked away from him. When I reached the flat, I threw myself down on the bed and cried, torrents and torrents of sickly, fat tears that made my head ache and shrivelled my skin into red buds. I stared at myself in the mirror. I looked alien. I was not the person I recognised. I was somebody else, somebody capable of uprooting and flying away, simply, as easy as that. The Angel I knew could not do this. So who was I? My world was no longer there. I had somehow managed to sweep the rug out from under my own feet. The flat spun around me incomprehensibly. The only thing I could do was finish my packing, and then, the tears all dried and my face forced into an image of strength and normality, drag my things out and quietly close the door behind me.

> You leave the railway station and wander up the street. All about the station and stretching away to the left, is a wilderness of small dull houses, built of sickly coloured yellow brick, pretending to look like stone – and roofed with thin, purple coloured slates. They cry out at you at the first glance, 'Workmen's houses' and a kind of instinct whispers to you 'Railway workmen and engineers'. Bright as the spring morning is, a kind of sick feeling of hopeless disgust comes over you, and you go on further, sure at any rate, that you cannot fare worse.

So wrote William Morris in 1885. His first images of the city were very similar to my own. I am not really sure where I went after I stepped off the train, but I do know that I walked for a very long time, until my feet were sore and my arms tired of pulling along my worldly possessions. The sunshine, unlike Morris's, was not bright, but I certainly felt the hopelessness he described. Perhaps that was why I stayed there. I think I might have found the spirit of the town suited to my gloomy mood and indeed my whole angle on life at that point. In any case, I had got off the train and I did not have the heart to get on another one and travel still further.

The first thing I did after I found somewhere to stay was to telephone my parents. I knew that both Alan and Justin would be worried about me, and that both Alan and Justin had my parents' phone number and would use it, and I wanted not only to inform my parents of what I had done, but also to prepare them for the calls they would inevitably receive. I don't think they understood me, and I had to explain to them about Alan, which was difficult, but I knew they would be on my side. I don't remember making many phone calls that long, not even those of the last few weeks, those soft-spoken night-time calls to Joe. They wanted to know everything. Despite an obvious disapproval, at another abrupt end to my education more than anything else, I think they were impressed. I told them how I had staggered on to the train and eventually ended up at the sun-soaked city of Peterborough. I told them how I had found a room, and they expressed concern at this. 'Angel, what would you have done if you weren't so lucky?' I gave them a list of things to say to Alan and to Justin, and firm instructions not to reveal my whereabouts. There were a number of things I did not tell them.

I have not told anyone how I sat right at the back of the train, leaning against the wall, just at the point where it would have been window anywhere else in the train, with my nose pressed into the cream-coloured plastic and the tears streaming down my cheeks, my neck and my breasts. No one knows about the kind but unwelcome words of the guard who came to check my ticket, almost guiltily.

'Are you okay, love?' he asked, with an intonation that matched the words in their straight-out-of-fiction character – I had never expected to find them anywhere in real life. It was embarrassing, not only because I was alone in a public place bawling my eyes out, but also because of the direly clichéd hue of the whole episode. I tried to answer in the affirmative, but I could not stem my stupid tears for a sufficient amount of time, so I merely nodded my head.

'Well, if you need anything, just give us a shout,' continued the thin, elderly voice.

After he left the carriage, my tears began anew, and I contemplated turning back. No one would know; it had not been long enough for anyone to miss me, and if I went back now the whole thing would merely have been a schizophrenic episode that, in time, I might convince myself had been a dream. A nightmare. Looking back on those days, I can even convince myself that the last two months have been spent in comparative luxury. However, looking back at those days is something that I do not like to do. I can still make myself miss Alan, and even Justin, in the moments when I am weak enough to try.

I had never been particularly enamoured with the dismal face of Manchester, and its innards were no better. There was something very frightening about the concrete buildings that looked as though their shapes had been forced up out of the plasticine ground by somebody on the other side pushing up a gigantic box. There was no landscape, no skyline, just an endless series of dead and dying buildings and greyness, even on the rare occasions when the rain stopped and the sun shone on the city. I am not sorry to have left it behind, and yet it was an important part of my life, and I regret that I cannot go back for that reason alone. The reality is that I could go back, any time I wanted to, but I can never recapture those days. They are days that I do not want to get back – but still, I resent the finality.

I did not choose Peterborough. I did not anticipate getting off there until the train began to slow among the Post Office buildings and catalogue warehouses that lurked along the skirts of the railway line. I had thought that maybe I would go on to London, slink across the underground like a hunted rat, and then get on a shiny train to the South Coast, to the sea: Brighton, Portsmouth, Lyme Regis. Then maybe I would get on a boat, hop across the Solent to the Isle of Wight perhaps, on a boat or a hovercraft. No, I must go further – the Channel Islands, France, Germany, Russia. And then my ridiculous thoughts were interrupted by the sound of the brakes, and I realised that it did not make any difference how far I went, just as long as it was out of sight of my present life – my old life, I reminded myself. As the box-patterned, square towers of the old Baker Perkins building loomed up at me, I gathered my things together. The train made the usual *shwooshing* and *clanking* noises as it came to a stop, and I dragged my luggage out on to the platforms of my Brave New World.

Depression is something that punches you in the stomach. It finds its way into you, imperceptibly through your defences, and entwines itself around you. It eats away at your body, your spirit, your mind, like a cancer. The primary tumour sits in your stomach, paining you, refusing to let you eat, allowing you neither rest nor sleep. It twists itself inside you, burrows further and further into you, and all the time you think it is at your very core, but still it can always dig deeper. It is a glowing spot, a fire, which turns you inside out and makes you realise that there is more space on the inside of you than there is surrounding you on the outside; more depths to be found by tunnelling, tunnelling through you than there is air and blue sky and twinkling stars in the entire universe. Sometimes you can feel the poisonous tendrils working their black magic through your veins, invading you, violating you, raping you.

Almost as soon as I had arranged my things in my room, paid my first rent cheque and filled my fridge with artefacts from the Co-op, it attacked me, vigorously, from every side, making a mockery of any defences I thought I had. I had been strong enough to make the initial move, but this had sapped me of all my energy, and I had none left with which to hold my fort. I knew I could not go back to Manchester and, although I missed my friends and my studies already, I did not really want to go back. It was not that; I was simply finished. I had nothing now. There was enough money in my bank account to last me for a month or so if I was careful, by which time I hoped to have a job, and I knew that my parents would always help out if I was in dire trouble, but still, I had nothing. No trade, no profession, no friends, no man by my side.

I thought about ringing some of my fellow students, now ex-fellow students, but I knew that even if I only spoke to one person they would coax me into giving my address, and soon everyone would know. I did not sleep at all on that first night. I cried into my duvet. I glared at all the things I had brought with me – the things that, only last night, had been happily arranged in the flat I shared with Justin in Manchester, and were now in this strange, cold room. I hated the wallpaper. The shapes were supposed to be flowers, but in my gloom they looked like strange beetles, or perhaps spiders, climbing the walls, and I felt they would reach the ceiling and crawl above my bed, finally springing on me in the darkness. So I kept the light on, and worried about the number of fifty pences I would have to put in the meter.

Dusk, then the blackness of complete night passed, and then slowly the day began to dawn outside my window, and I crept over to see the sun rise. Outside the panes I saw a wide, grey road flanked on either side with oblong patches of square grass, separated by the prongs of people's driveways. Immediately outside the house I was in and the three or four pairs of similar council-type houses surrounding it, there were no dropped kerbs, and the grass stretched out comparatively expansively. In my mind I pictured children playing here, and the thought dismayed me. I was alone and depressed and the last thing I wanted to see was other people enjoying themselves. A few trees were scattered about the place. Even at this hour I could sense the humidity of the day forming around me, and I knew their leaves would be heavy with the hot teardrops of sweat by the time noon arrived.

I crawled back into bed and lay with my hands beneath my head. The rays of sunshine mosaicked over me like fragments of all the different people I seemed to have become. I let them play with my feelings, let them shake me around and take me back to all the places I had been in my life, and I think I slept for a short time, because it was soon eight o'clock, and I heard people in the rooms around me beginning to stir. I went once more to the window. By nine the place was silent again, and I was still staring out of the window. It suddenly occurred to me that people might have seen me, and I quickly hid myself on the room side of the curtain. There was my room, cold and alien, completely different in the daylight. It had been dark before I got there the night before, and my need to find a place to stay had been so urgent that I took the room because the rent was not too high and it was a reasonable size. In the gloom and panic of that evening there had not been any other considerations. I suppose I was lucky that I did not end up somewhere much worse, considering the tiny amount of effort I put into finding my new residence, but I could not help comparing it with the comfortable flat I had just left. The tears threatened to fall, but I think that I had shed too many already. I was dried up, and I was thankful for this.

I wonder what Bryony would have thought of Peterborough. It can perhaps describe itself as cosmopolitan, having shifted around in its time between four different counties: those of Lincolnshire, Northamptonshire, Huntingdonshire and finally Cambridgeshire, where it presently resides. I close my eyes and picture myself taking her hand and leading her off the train into the sprawling mixture of new and old, clean and dirty, functional and decorative. I would take her to see the old pub that is surrounded on three sides by the orange-brown brick and gasping windows of the shopping centre which clasps it at the left and right and looms up behind it. The pale bricks and dormer windows barely manage to hold their own; it is an anachronism, truly, and as such it is ugly, yet it is fascinating that the town planners found it so necessary to preserve it.

I would have tugged at her arm and pulled her to the river embankment that somehow manages to be peaceful despite being in the middle of the city. We would have sat on the wooden benches in the shadow of the riverside theatre, and I would have made her gasp by telling her how those same benches were almost completely underwater in some floods once, only the two longer posts at the back corners appearing out of the murky water for air. We might stay there until it got dark and perhaps walk a little further along the river, underneath the sweeping noise of the Parkway and into the comparative countryside, where all around us would be black. We would have looked back at the glow from the cathedral, standing tall in all its glory amongst the stars.

Perhaps I would have taken her inside one day and shown her the grave of Catherine of Aragon, or taken her further afield to Fotheringhay where the body of Mary Queen of Scots was allowed to lie for some twenty-five years. My lips curve into a wry smile at the thought that not even dead people can bear to remain in Peterborough for too long, both of these queens having been eventually removed for burial elsewhere.

I studied the map I had bought myself at the station in an attempt to work out where I was, and discovered that, despite my endless walking last night, I was just a few small minutes from the station. It was still looming there, big in my life, threatening to take me back and render my escape ineffective. It had sucked me in towards it when I thought I was going further and further away; dragged me back in evil spirals. I had not undressed for the night, so, in the same clothes I had been wearing when I let Justin kiss me goodbye, when I had coffee with Alan, when I sat on the train letting it carry me wherever its whims might lead it, I walked out into the sunshine and made my way into the town centre. I crossed the railway line and thought about the previous day.

I had to remind myself who I was; once again, I did not think I was a person who could take such a drastic action. Justin would, of course, know by now that I was gone, and would almost certainly have spoken to my parents and learned the truth. I wondered how he must be feeling: alone, distraught, offended... I did not know. He knew as well as I did that our relationship had become a sham, and I wondered if he might also be secretly relieved that I had provided him with an effort-free way out. Then I thought of Alan. He would not yet know. Our relationship had been constantly on a knife-edge; sometimes we had been together almost continuously for days on end, and at other times it had not been possible to see him for long periods. I wondered how long it would be before he realised that he was not going to see me again. I almost wanted to telephone him, to say goodbye properly, but I restrained myself. I had made my grand gesture, and crawling back to that life, from however great a distance, would be to throw the whole effort back into my own face.

I had to peer at the map to find out where I had got to. If I looked over the side of the bridge I could see the archaic industrial buildings that I had noticed when the train began to slow there the previous day. I recognised the noughts and crosses pattern on the side of the pink concrete, the slitted windows. Here and there a window space was covered with thick, rough board, and the whole place looked to be in a state of disrepair. To my right was the road section of the bridge, separated from the footpath by a high wall; but if I stood on my toes and craned a little, I could make out, just a few steps along the track, the station. On a vertical level with me was the vulgar bridge I had spotted on leaving the train yesterday. It was high and crescent-shaped, and painted bright blue and dark red. I was able to work out from the map where I was now – assuming that the hideous bridge was, true to its shape, the one marked on the map as Crescent Bridge. I had come a bit of a long way round, but was heading in roughly the right direction.

A large toy shop. A gleaming McDonalds. Petrol stations, a fire station, complete with ludicrous training tower, a road named a Boulevard, although it looked nothing whatsoever like one. And then finally a meccano bridge across the airless dual carriageway leading into what looked from the outside like an enormous multi-storey car park, but ingeniously had a shopping centre hidden inside it. Queensgate must have sparkled once but I found it somehow lacking in enthusiasm. I dodged my way through the mirrored pillars and found myself in the sunshine of Cathedral Square. A few more tears squeezed themselves out from somewhere far behind my eyes, and a few more people stared at me, but I did not care. Then a miracle; around a corner stood a majestic stone arch, ripples of layers hanging from the solid main structure. Inside all I could see was paving and grass, but above it I could see the pale spires of the cathedral. It was beautiful, but there was no point in being happy.

Rivergate looked tired and sorry. I found the market, and also that it sold nothing I wanted, not knowing that it would become such a large part of my life a few weeks on. I wandered the streets for most of that day, sometimes crying, sobbing, sometimes not, but always with this monster in my stomach. I felt that the world was falling in around me, closing itself in at me, four walls – no, more – moving at me like the obligatory scene from so many James Bond films. There was just no point. I felt this more than I felt anything else. We spend our lives getting through each day in the blind hope that tomorrow will be better. Now, for the first time, I had lost this hope. I knew, for certain, that this was as good as I could ever expect to feel.

I knew that even when 'good things' happened, I was not happy, and I began to weigh everything up in my mind. I had no idea where I would go after I died, or whether I would still exist. So that was not an entity I had any control over – it was a dreadful, black unknown. All I knew was that I could endure sixty years of misery and then die, or I could die now. Either way, I had death to contend with, but in one case I could do without the misery beforehand. I knew I would never kill myself. I knew I was far too weak for that, unfortunately, and this contributed to the depression by forcing me to concede that there was no way out.

Sometimes I considered going back to Justin. I had not been happy there, but I had never reached these depths. I knew, though, that it was too late; going back now would not mean that these weeks had never happened, and I knew I would always be aware that I had failed. Justin was not too tempting an option, but it was Alan who almost felled me. Every day I wondered whether or not he had missed me yet. Every morning when I woke up I had to prepare myself for yet another day without him. It was a long time before I really believed that I would not see him again, that he was no longer a part of my life. I pictured him sometimes, sitting cross-legged on his bed, watching me undress. I saw him in lectures, the weight of concentration heavily on his shoulders. I missed him. I worked hard to convince myself that it was not Alan I had been in love with, but the whole idea of being wanted, lusted for, that wonderful sensation of new love, and perhaps even the concept of infidelity.

The clasp of new hands, the fuzz of mutual desire; desire much the stronger for being yet unfulfilled, feeding on the very frustration it fuels. It is a circle; the challenge is to wait as long as can be borne before plunging in, rippling the already storm-ridden waters, making something comprehensible of the violent, senseless patterns. Then the second test begins; when the water becomes still, it is at an end.

Is this where I am with Joe? During those days with Bryony I thought it was, but I cannot seem to keep a thought still in my mind for more than a moment. I am looking forward to going home to him. I can hardly wait to be in his arms, to be loved and kissed by him and to feel his need for me. Perhaps this is because I miss Bryony, because I am lonely now, or perhaps it is because I never really stopped wanting Joe. Bryony made my life a different colour for those hazy weeks, and reality became obscured for a short while. This is not to say that I did not want Bryony. I know that I did, but I am no longer sure that I wanted *only* Bryony.

Perhaps I have grown up enough in the last few weeks to have realised that I must work hard to avoid this stasis with Joe. It is where a relationship ends and it requires all of one's efforts to keep it at bay. It is not enough to tumble into the well of a relationship, your fall broken by the soft cushions of novelty and lust. When these are drawn from under you, as they inevitably are, you are left with a hard concrete floor which you cannot endure for long, and the climb out is a difficult one.

But now I am not sure if I want to climb out of the well I am in with Joe. I know that the floor will not remain soft, is changing, hardening; but perhaps the key is for me to change with it, so that I no longer need to be cushioned by the things a fickle woman might crave. Instead, my buttocks are forming a hard, protective shell so that I may sit here for ever and feel no pain. There is a whole concrete life with Joe stretching out before me if I choose to take it. Will I prefer it over the transitoriness of plush, velvety cushions? It is a difficult decision to make. We cannot build our houses out of cushions, can we?

Making love with him will be different, I am sure, but still as delicious as I remember. There is a circle drawing itself around me, I think, or perhaps I am the ink with which it is being drawn. As my train pulled out of Durham Station that morning, my skin was prickling with the need for him. I thought I would miss him more and more as time went by, but then I met Bryony and she went some way towards filling that need in me. Or rather, she didn't fill the need, but created a new one, which masked the old one and rendered it insignificant. Now she has died and left a different hole in me, and it is no less vivid than my need for Joe, but it has passed somehow into a different realm. I think I wanted Joe all along. To feel his strong arms around my waist, his soft lips making little indentations in my skin as he traces a pattern of kisses over me, the hard cone of his crotch exploding out into the thick air as I unbutton his trousers.

Then I will perhaps stand in the kitchen and bake him cakes, little cakes with songs in them, as the songs of love and fascination I sing drop some of their fragments into the mixture. It is a ludicrous image but a very concrete one: four walls and a solid roof, a doorbell and a cake mixer. I am not sure if it is an image that fits in with my life, but then again, perhaps you have to take your life and fit it in with the images in your head. If I had taken Bryony, I would have shattered those conventional images, making life all new for myself, and I would have needed to pluck new images out of somewhere. I didn't think of that at the time. It felt so natural and so necessary to love her. It still feels natural and necessary to love her, and still, my grief and my loss are mingled with a sense of joy at the feelings she has awakened in me. All over, I am blooming with new buds and fresh green leaves, even though she has left them to wilt and die as soon as they burst out.

My journey must be almost at an end. The blues and purples of lavender are giving way to burnished red poppies and bright yellow mustard – the native crops of my new home town. My eyes wander out into the middle of the long grass where the poppies waver in the wind, and I think of taking Joe by the hand and leading him into the field. We would find a nook, a corner, somewhere quiet, where I would perform skilful fellatio on him. He would roll his eyes in ecstasy, and afterwards, we would play amongst the poppies like children.

Home

Durham Station approaches. That familiar skyline that I was so loath to leave and now anticipate with some trepidation. The sun has grown brighter, and although the day is nearly at an end, it shines its swansong rays with all the effort it can muster. I know that Joe will be in the kitchen, cooking for me, having timed everything perfectly so that he can leave it for just the amount of time it will take to pick me up from the station, and I feel genuine, utter delight at the thought. Caterpillars and a few butterflies begin to create havoc in my stomach as the train slows, almost to a halt, still moving long after I feel it should have stopped. For a moment I panic and think that the train will not stop here, that it will take me away from home, having brought me so close, but eventually the brakes hiss, the doors open and I am on the platform.

He takes my face between his palms and draws me towards him. Closing his eyes, he kisses me, eagerly, passionately, as if trying to make up for all those long weeks spent apart. He has missed me, I know this – so much, it has left him with a gaping hole in his stomach. He has thought about me night and day. He has knelt on his bed at home in the evenings – the bed where I should have been – closed his eyes, and pictured me there beneath him, hard as he was with desire for me, desire which was only ever partially fulfilled while he was away from me. All this I can read in this face, his actions, his kisses.

But now I am here, and I have missed him too, more than I have dared to realise, despite everything. I close my eyes and feel the passion in his kiss. I think of all those nights in my bare hotel room, of how my body ached for him continuously, of all the times I imagined him naked in my bed, while I lay there alone, alone and sad. I have not reflected these times in my reminiscing; they seemed so irrelevant when all I could think about was Bryony, and my love for her, and my loss. I suppose they were insignificant then, but now that I am with him he has the power to make them large again. We look deeply at each other. I love the way his hair hangs down around his face, I love his bright, loving eyes, the feel of his arms tightly about me. Happy, I nestle my face into his neck, kiss him gently there, and let myself be buried in his presence. For a moment it is as though none of the crazy things I experienced have happened to me at all, as though I am waking from a vivid dream, safe in my bed. I surprise myself: this is genuine. I thought I would feel all these things, but only by an act of will, yet here they are, love for Joe, lust for Joe, the ecstasy of being close to him again, and they have flown upon me unaided.

I wonder what would have happened had Bryony returned to me on the evening of her death, had she not fallen into lifelessness on the plush carpet. We had already spent one night together, albeit by accident through our tiredness and drunkenness, but there was a definite sense of something imminent and significant floating around us. If I believed in such things, I might say it was a forewarning of her death that had touched me on the shoulder, but I know it was not that. There was a straining in the air around us, formed perhaps from the efforts of us both to control our lust for each other, although neither of us really wanted to. Perhaps the alcohol that Bryony had gone to fetch would have given us both the strength and the fading out of reality to take things further.

I still do not know what 'further' would have meant. I cannot imagine making love with Bryony; but then I never imagined making love with Joe before it happened. Sex is something you don't intend to do, but when the kissing starts, the stroking, the caressing, all of which you have intended, there is often no stopping. Until then, the breathlessness, the whimpering, the whining, the grinding of each into the other that you have felt before and that you know sex to consist of, is unimaginable. Perhaps you crave intimacy. Perhaps you want to kiss, to caress, but you never expect to fuck. Then he or she touches you and your body leaps into life. Your breathing turns to gasps, you no longer have control over it, and you press yourself into your partner, wildly, desperately, in a way that would embarrass you deeply were you to think about it in the cold light of day. And you never more will think of it in this way; once it has happened, you cannot imagine it without the deep, intense pleasure that seemed so natural, and you cannot feel awkward.

This is certainly how it has always happened to me in the past. It is the closeness and the tenderest of physical contact that I crave. I suppose the human body is constructed to burst into flames at the slightest touch, the slightest hint that reproduction may be possible. We are programmed to continue our own species, after all. I am sure that if Bryony had touched me in the same way that Joe is touching me now, in a way that showed me that the innermost thoughts in her mind were the same as mine, that her fantasies were as mine, I would have reacted in much the same way; I would have crossed that tenuous line and found myself within the boundaries of pure, unadulterated adultery.

I feel his arm around my waist begin to lead me out of the door and to his car, and, after stopping to kiss him once more, I eventually walk out of the station with him. Now that I am back, with him again, I want to heave his body on to the floor, there amid the orange cycle stands and the weeds sprouting up from the holes in the concrete, and I picture this in my mind as I climb into the car. A corner of my skirt falls away and he seizes the opportunity to place a hand on my leg. We both sigh like wound up clockwork, and I pull him towards me by the hair in order to kiss him again. He slides his hand further up my leg, high inside my skirt, and I whisper something unintelligible through the kiss.

Oh, Bryony, I feel as though I am about to commit a dreadful sin. I know that I will make love with Joe when we get home. I knew all along that I would, but I expected to hate it, to need to force myself. It is not like that. His familiar touch, his comforting voice, I cannot but need him. I promised myself that I was yours. I promised you that I was yours, even though you were not there to hear me, and I meant it. And yet I am being unfaithful already. I turn my head to look out of the side window, and then I close my eyes and try to fill my nostrils with your scent, but it is Joe, all around me, and I cannot make him vanish, not for a moment. I want to cry and batter the dashboard with my poor grieving hands, and yet I cannot.

We pull up into the driveway, and he smiles at me and leads me swiftly towards the front door. There was not even time to get a key cut before I left, so he lets me in, and I can feel him watching my eyes dart around the room, seeing what a good job he has made with the house. He must have worked hard to arrange it; I picture him attempting to guess what I would have done, what I would find pleasing. He has even arranged flowers, almost certainly fresh that morning, in an enormous translucent burgundy vase in the hallway. He looks at me, as though his eyes are wondering whether I am still the same beneath my clothes, whether I will still melt at his touch over the curves of my body. I am still the same beneath my clothes; but am I the same beneath my skin?

Bryony's plain black top, tight but not clingy, drawing an oval beneath her neck and two more around her wrists. Her skirt was long and intricately patterned, and she wore loose brown sandals on her feet. I watched the way the black material stretched and loosened over her breasts as she rocked backward and forward, her arms cradling her ankles, on her bed. I thought so hard about tracing that outline with a finger that I fancied I could almost feel it; her soft, springy flesh beneath my fingertip, upwards to her firm collarbone and then above the line of the fabric to her naked neck. Perhaps I would have protruded my finger very slightly underneath the black material and just traced the line of it, touched her skin only very lightly. Perhaps she would have clasped her arms around me at the sensation, drawn lines up and down my back with her own fingers, rested her hands on my shoulders, and then maybe she would have drawn me towards her and kissed me.

The table is set with a new tablecloth and a few candles. He has tried hard, but I almost laugh at the cliché. We go through into the kitchen, and he grabs my waist and pulls me suddenly against him. I throw my head back for him to kiss my neck, and he obliges. The sauce is bubbling in the pan, and he expertly stirs it while continuing to kiss me. I take a deep breath. Joe, Bryony is dead. I have said it in my head, but not out loud. The words would sound so artificial. He would wonder, too, at the signifi- cance I know I would express in them, and I cannot say them. I try something else. Joe, I was in love with Bryony. *Was* in love with her? I am still deeply in love with her, and yet how can I say *am* when she is dead? His mouth moves from my neck to my chin, and then swiftly and seamlessly to my lips, where he kisses me deeply.

The pasta is drained and served and the sauce poured gaily on top. We sit at the table and mechanically spoon it into our mouths. I wonder why he did not plan to take me to bed before we ate, but I am glad he did not. I don't think I am ready to feel him inside me yet, even though I suddenly desire it, crave it. I feel as though my head is in a throbbing mess, and I want to give it time to calm down.

'Joe, there is something I really need to tell you.'

'What's wrong?'

'It's Bryony.' He would be puzzled at this stage, but would continue to listen with his concerned face.

What would I tell him first? I would need to impart both pieces of information simultaneously, but this would be impossible. Would I garble, 'I fell in love with her but now she is dead'? The words seem so small and insignificant. I continue to chew the pasta, swallowing with some difficulty because of the pregnant bulge in my throat. 'Bryony... she died. She had a brain haemorrhage and just died on the spot.'

He would be speechless. He has not, of course, met her, but he has heard plenty about her, although this had become less and less as time went by; the closer I was to her, the less I wanted Joe to know about her.

'I'm okay,' I would lie. 'I've been upset, but I'm getting over it.' And then, softly, quietly, 'I fell in love with her.'

I hear the words with my mind but not my ears, and I wait to see if I can conjure up his reaction. Impossible.

Our spoons and forks screech over the emptying plates as we scoop up the last of the sauce. There is a large sticky chocolate pudding for dessert, but before I am allowed to eat it, he leans over the table and offers me his lips, which I gladly move towards and kiss. It is delicious to kiss Joe. I don't think it matters what is going on even millimetres from our lips when we are kissing. Our lips withdraw from one another's, and we begin to devour the pudding. The feel of the sponge between my teeth is soft and comforting, and the chocolate sauce wends its way slippily down my throat. My foot touches Joe's underneath the table, and he looks at me with narrowed eyes. I know what is coming and I am no longer frightened.

Meandering up the stairs to our bedroom, drawn to the heat of the blazing fire that rages in the antique fireplace, I turn to him and begin to compliment him on his success with the house, but before any words come out, he thanks me, proudly, with a smile, and then kisses me into silence. I grab the back of his head and pull him hard against me, so that he can kiss me still more deeply. For a long, long time we kiss, and then our hands begin to journey over each other's bodies. It is as though this is new. We have been apart for so long that we are almost unfamiliar to each other. Our breathing is deepening, little cries escaping every now and again, our bodies tingling. I can feel his impatient desire almost as intensely as my own – my own unwanted and yet so welcome desire.

In the moments of anticipation before we make love, my brain throbs with images and sensations of things I had forgotten I wanted. My body was last touched by Bryony; affectionately, warmly, not sexually, yet touched. The last time I kissed someone it was a dead woman. I feel as though I only experienced those days and weeks in a dream, or as though they happened to someone else, and suddenly, all that matters is the here and now. Almost without me noticing, we have begun to make love. I am never sure at what point the line between foreplay and sex is crossed, but I am aware that we have crossed it now. I had forgotten the insistent rhythm of lovemaking, the slow beginning, slow and deeply sensual, the creeping inevitability of climax, the feel of his skin against mine, the sticky sweat building up on my brow. And then, finally, deliciously, my body becomes inextricably joined with my soul and also with his body, and all I can do is cling to him and let the immense waves pass over me.

Flicking my eyes open with the force of the pleasure, the death-like qualities of the orgasm, I find myself staring into the fireplace. The orange flames are dancing themselves into spikes, burning stalagmites, and they draw my eyes toward them. My body tightens as the image of another fire flashes into my mind; a long forgotten and obscurely misted over image, which for a moment I have to struggle to stabilise before I can see it all.

★

Marcus is crying, 'Hot, really hot!' in what he intends to be a stern, authoritative voice, and our brother is collapsing into fits of giggles. I can feel the fire burning behind me as I desperately and in vain peep into the old coal scuttle. I walk around the fire, red shoes scattering the debris, finding silvery ashes, singed paper covered in what is left of newsprint, unrecognisable parts of now unrecognisable vegetables, grasses and leaves and roots. And then the charred remains of my beautiful cat. The shock: the pain, the anger, the nausea.

★

In this instant, it all flies back into my consciousness, and astringent tears roll down my cheeks. Joe must be concerned at these tears, and holds me more tightly still, his breathing fast and deep. Confusion overtakes me, and suddenly, with the exhaustion of a spent lover and a heady tiredness from too much thinking, all I want to do is sleep. He whispers, 'I love you,' and, my body still racked with the receding waves of orgasm, my psyche struggling with the sudden surge of self-knowledge, I sleep.

I awake to find myself safely in my lover's arms, and feign continued sleep as the moment is too delicious to break. He strokes my cheek with his hand and kisses my hair that is lying on the pillow. He lets his hand continue down to my neck, my collarbone, and runs it over my breast. I feel my nipple harden under his fingers, and stir, roll my head on the pillow and sigh happily. Perhaps the part of my brain that stores unwanted memories is full. Perhaps it took a much worse experience to bring out the lesser one. Now that I have so many images of Bryony's death and the events surrounding it to tuck away in the darkness out of sight, there is no room for my memory of my cat, and I have had to pull it out into the brightness of my consciousness. Is this the way it works? It seems unlikely and yet I cannot but feel that I have exchanged an old memory for a new one.

Were Alan and Justin the real reasons I left Manchester? Was it all just an excuse, a carefully concocted conspiracy with my subconscious that enabled me to throw away something I wanted yet again? Perhaps I would have become suspicious had I gone on throwing things away with no ostensible reason. Was it just my own way of convincing myself to take a step that I had already decided upon? Bryony is the only thing I have lost involuntarily since the cat. I look back through my life, struggling to find something that has been lost against my will, but can find nothing. All my losses have had an element of will in them.

Perhaps history works even harder than I thought. One small afternoon in my life, and the whole of its course is irreversibly changed. And it is a history I didn't even know about. I consider questioning my parents to find out if it is really true, but decide that it is better off in my head the way I have remembered it. Aristotle thought that the truth of history was inferior to the fictions of literature, and I think he was right. If I have not remembered it correctly in my head, it doesn't matter. And I feel as though I have told Joe about Bryony, even though the conversation only occurred in my head. Maybe that is acceptable, since there was nothing illicit, nothing questionable between us other than in my head. Perhaps I should leave the whole matter there, where it begun and where it has stayed so far.

I love Joe. And I came so close to giving him up. I know that I was carried off with Bryony on the whirl of my loneliness, the magic of Beethoven, the excitement of the love I know she felt for me, and yet that does not make my love appear any less intense. If a person is really made up from their past, what happens when that past changes as rapidly and as crazily as mine has in the last two months? Am I still the same person, or have my experiences made me someone new?

I was wrong about journeys. I thought that it was possible for them to end, that you could finish them and stay in one place, but now I realise that you cannot. We are always going, always going somewhere, always leaving somewhere else, by trains, buses, aeroplanes, trams, by bicycle, on foot. It is inevitable. It will always be the case. Nothing in the universe is ever still.

Bryony and I were never lovers. Had we had more time, or more courage, we might have been. I do not know whether or not she would have liked us to be, but despite everything, I know that I feel no regret for the things that did happen, both in reality and in my mind (if there is a difference). I was very close to leaving Joe for her. I have learned a lot about myself, and about the world, on this course – more training than they could ever have hoped to provide me with, and at more expense than they will ever imagine.

I feel cruel. I know that I loved Bryony and that I will continue to love her for the rest of my life, but I suddenly feel I can begin to get on with that life, to get back to my life the way it was before this brief but intensely educational experience. I do not know what would have happened if she had still been alive, but I am not going to let myself use that as an excuse to throw away something else that I have and want passionately. And I do want it passionately; despite Bryony, despite all my deepest worries. I know that Joe is something that I *Want*.

The fire smoulders in the grate, dying away, a few vaguely orange embers struggling to survive but irreversibly dying. Soon they will all be gone. The irony is that it has taken the loss of Bryony for me to learn all this. Had she not died, I would not have been able to take her – for I am sure now that it is my love for her and her death that have forced out my cat reminiscences – because I would not have learnt to take the things that I want. But now that I know what to do, I cannot do it because she is gone. I wish I could reach back into the past, knowing what I know now, and clasp her firmly against me, somehow save her, ensure that I did not lose her either voluntarily or involuntarily. But alas, that is against the nature of history.

At the same time, I am determined not to enforce loss upon myself again. I know that my life with Joe is mine for the taking and I decide that I will take it. Joe can make me happy, I know that now. I also know that everything I felt for Bryony will never leave my head, or indeed my heart. It will be my secret knowledge, my secret love affair, and as I go through my life with Joe she will always be here, with me, more real perhaps than she would have been had she lived. I will go through my life on a double-edged sword; when I am not with Joe, I will be with her, I will know the deep-cutting pleasure of what it is like to love and be loved by her. Bryony might not have given me what I wanted in life: there would always have been men, or time, or geographical barriers; but in death, she is mine.